Messengers
from the Vernal Wood

First International Youth Poetry Festival
Special Session for BRICS Countries

Compiled by *Poetry Periodical*

青春，如风有信

首届国际青春诗会——金砖国家专场

《诗刊》社 / 编

International Youth Poetry Festival

First Edition 2024

ISBN 978-7-119-14038-4
© Foreign Languages Press Co. Ltd, Beijing, China, 2024
Published by Foreign Languages Press Co. Ltd
24 Baiwanzhuang Road, Beijing 100037, China
Distributed by China International Book Trading Corporation
35 Chegongzhuang Xilu, Beijing 100044, China
P.O. Box 399, Beijing, China

Printed in the People's Republic of China

Preface

Using the Power of Literature to Dredge the River of Communication between Human Civilizations

In ancient China, poets often gathered for various literary events, giving rise to numerous masterpieces through their interactions and exchanges. The deep friendships forged among these poets have been passed down through the ages, inspiring admiration. Since its establishment in 1980, the renowned poetry journal *Poetry Periodical*, hosted by the China Writers Association, has successfully organized 39 editions of the Youth Poetry Festival, making it the most influential and enduring literary gathering in China. Countless young poets have grown into pillars of the poetry world through this platform, while also forming lifelong friendships with one another. The First International Youth Poetry Festival - Special Session for BRICS Countries is a brand-new concept and grand vision that has emerged from the foundation of the Youth Poetry Festival. Now, we have the privilege of witnessing its journey onto the global stage, eagerly anticipating its mark in the history of international poetry exchanges.

Wang Bo, a renowned poet of China's Tang Dynasty, once penned the verse: "If you have friends who know your heart, distance cannot keep you apart." Though we are from diverse nations, separated by vast physical distances, poetry bridges our hearts and minds, forging a timeless connection. Poetry uplifts our spirits, ignites our souls, warms the earth, and gives voice to all living things. It stands as a radiant gem atop the crown of literature, transcending the barriers of time and geography, weaving tales of lives once distant and unfamiliar, and exploring the universal realm of human emotions and the rich tapestry of historical and cultural landscapes.

Poetry is like a vast and mighty canal of the spirit. Flowing endlessly, it creates a common language for people of different countries and ethnic groups, allowing diverse lives, emotions, cultures, and thoughts to collide and merge. Poetic dialogue allows us to understand, respect, and inspire each other. This is precisely the original intention of the China Writers Association in holding the First International Youth Poetry Festival - Special Session for BRICS Countries. We hope to use the power of literature to dredge the river of communication between human civilizations, deepen mutual understanding, and promote multicultural exchanges.

Throughout history, the Chinese people have greatly benefited from extensive and in-depth exchanges with other nations, and the cultural essence of various ethnic groups around the world has continuously injected new vitality into Chinese culture. At the same time, the influence of Chinese culture has also spread to all corners of the world. For foreign poets who have traveled all the way to China, the International Youth Poetry Festival may be brief, spanning just a few days. But I believe that the cultural tapestry of China, its breathtaking landscapes, rich history and profound humanity, will unveil a brilliance that will resonate deeply within you, even as you carry the memories of the vast world you have already explored. If this inspiration sparks a new flame in your writing, it will be a special gift from the Chinese people to you. We hope that you will take back home your understanding and appreciation of the Chinese culture and poetry, sharing it with your family and friends. Let us harness the power of poetry to forge bridges of communication between our hearts and minds and work together to build a better world for the mankind.

Wishing our poet friends eternal companionship with youth and wishing our poetry eternal youth.

(Excerpt from the speech at the opening ceremony of the First International Youth Poetry Festival—Special Session for BRICS Countries delivered by Mr. Zhang Hongsen, Secretary of the Party Leadership Group and Vice President of China Writers Association on July 19th, 2024)

序 言

用文学的力量浚通人类文明的交流之河

在中国古代，诗人们经常举行各种形式的诗文雅集，很多名篇佳作就在诗人们的相互交流与酬酢中诞生，诗人之间的深厚友谊也被后人津津乐道。由中国作家协会主办的著名诗歌刊物《诗刊》自 1980 年创立青春诗会，已经成功举办了 39 届。这是中国影响力最大、持续时间最长的文学笔会。无数青年诗人经由它，成长为诗坛的中流砥柱，彼此之间也结成了一生的挚友。首届国际青春诗会——金砖国家专场正是在青春诗会基础上生长出来的一个全新的设想、宏伟的蓝图。现在，我们有幸在这里见证它走向世界，期待它在国际诗歌交流史上留下浓墨重彩的一笔。

中国唐代诗人王勃有一句诗："海内存知己，天涯若比邻。"大家来自不同国家，从物理空间上看也许相隔遥远，但在心灵世界里，诗却让我们时时相通。诗歌使人精神欢愉，使灵魂发光，使天地温暖，使万物发声。它是文学桂冠上的明珠，能够超越历史与地理的阻隔，讲述那些原本遥远、陌生的生活，探索人类共通的情感世界和多元的历史文化空间。

诗歌就像一条浩浩汤汤、奔流不息的精神运河，它为不同国家、不同民族的人们创造出一种共同语言，使多元多样的生活、情感、文化、思想得以碰撞融汇。诗歌对话让我们能够相互理解、相互尊重、相互鼓舞。这也正是中国作家协会举办首届国际青春诗会——金砖国家专场的初衷。我们希望用文学的力量浚通人类文明的交流之河，加深相互了解、促进多元文化交流。

从古至今，中国人民在广泛而深入的对外交流中获益匪浅，世界各民族的文化精髓不断为中华文化注入新的生命活力。与此同时，中华文化的影响力也持续辐射到世界各地。对远道而来的外国诗人朋友来说，虽然国际青春诗会只有短短几天，但我相信，中国的山水风物、历史人文，即便在你们已经看过广阔世界的双眼中，也一定会绽放出别样的光彩。如果这种光彩能够在你们未来的写作道路上留下潜移默化的印迹，那么这就是中国人民送给你们的一份特别的礼物。也希望你们把自己对中国文化、中国诗歌的理解与感受带回故乡，分享给身边的亲友。用诗歌搭建起我们心灵的沟通之桥，携手并肩，共同建设人类的美好家园。

祝福诗人朋友们永远与青春同行，祝福我们的诗歌永远年轻。

（选自中国作家协会党组书记、副主席张宏森2024年7月19日在首届国际青春诗会——金砖国家专场开幕式上的致辞）

This Poem Is Dedicated to Us[*]

Birds sing at my window
Pectoral movements guide their flight
She begins to hunt for a direction
Dragon song still reverberating in her ears

Everyone swaps positions on the chessboard
Captivated by the gravity of words
I look for words unused by poets
How many times I have been a white rice paper
Creating new sounds from words each time
I choose to light up the paper
You make an easy form
Our stories produce parts interlaced
Women are the descendants of the sun
As a poem brims with meaning
This poem is dedicated to us
To my father, who is greater than the world

Far and far away, obscured by the noise
Giant root system of the plant hides great passion

---

[*] Note: This poem is jointly composed on the same topic by the Chinese
and foreign poets who participated in the 1st International Youth Poetry
Festival, consisting of 72 lines. A list of the authors of each part is attached
to the color foldout.

Nothing to ask for but this extensive peace
The boat gliding through the middle
I travel an endless life in fantasy
I use only torches to clarify the vowels
Worth standing on the summit of a poem
Please come together, dear star

When I jump at you like a child
Embracing under the extensive starry sky
I drink you from the honey of a smile
In the glimpse of twilight
Pave the way back
In the shoes of a river
I can finally sleep in peace
In the face of this profound world
The childish me inspires the middle-aged me
I pray for another me to fall
Don't turn on the light, your eyes will guide me

Across seaside hills, bushes and elephant land
To reach the edge of a mountain
When time-warped memories fall
You are the last fruit left on a crooked branch
For the unknown reader, finder or seeker
Touch the ever soft air
The fire of history closes its doors behind us
All things shine into our hearts

Every dawn, every dusk
And the plain in the distance overlooking us
Street lights come on one after another

Open the door to another life of light
As coming out of a grand light
I will return to you in the form of a river bed

Burning words, bells
Almost everything that can be seen is reborn
I am an ignorant student in this infinite space and time
Let us reunite to be born again
Let us invite the whole world to fall in perfect snow
Listen to the snow falling into the urn of time
Recite to an invisible audience

Sometimes gifts speak for us
The moon stuck high in the sky
Love swims in her abandoned garden
Floating on a boat with no name
Please respect my traditional orientation
The light before dawn
Over the faint flames

Here is an oud, no one playing
A million words hidden in the sand
Take your seeds and your faith
Write another line after many years
Until one day, thoughts like waves
Praise the water in a girl's eyes
Happiness gets shape in sharing
The melody sounds softly and sets the mood
It plays for every moment of my life

(English translation: Hai An & Jin Jin)

"首届国际青春诗会 —— 金砖国家专场"
诗人同写一首诗

这首诗献给我们*

在我的窗前鸟儿歌唱
肩膀的运动引导飞翔
她开始寻找一个方向
龙吟在耳边依旧回响

每个人都在棋盘上改变位置
被词汇的魔力吸引
我寻找诗人未曾写过的语词
多少次我是一张洁白的宣纸
让词语每一次都产生新的声音
我选择照亮纸
你制造轻易的形式
我们的故事产生部分交错
女人是太阳的后裔
像一首充满意义的诗
这首诗献给我们
献给我的父亲，他比世界还要壮丽

辽远，被喧嚣掩映
植物庞大的根系藏着巨大的激情

---

* 注：此诗为参加首届国际青春诗会的中外诗人们同题联合创作。全诗72行，
每句诗的作者名单谨附于彩色折页之后。

别无所求，除了这辽阔的宁静
船从中间穿过滑行
我在幻想中游历漫长的生命
只用火把将元音阐明
值得站在一首诗的峰顶
请靠拢并齐，亲爱的星星

当我如孩子般扑向你
拥抱在辽阔的星空下
我正从一道笑容的蜂蜜中饮你
在夕阳的余光里
重铺回归之路
在河的鞋子里
终于可以安然入睡
面对着世事深邃
幼稚的我激励中年的我
我祈愿天空落下另一个我
不要开灯，你的双眼就可以指引我

越过海边山丘，灌木丛和大象之地
到一处山麓的边缘，在那里
当记忆在时间弯曲中变得恍惚
你是弯曲的树枝上最后剩下的果实
为了未知的读者，探路人或求索者
触摸永远柔和的空气
历史之火在我们身后关上大门
万物流萤照进我们心底

每个黎明，每个黄昏
还有在远方的平原俯瞰我们
街灯一盏接一盏亮起

开启通往另一世光明的门
像从巨大的光明中走出
我将以河床的形式回归你

灼热的话语，钟声
所有能看见的几乎都是新生
我是这无垠时空中懵懂的学生
让我们重新结合以获重生
邀请整个世界完完整整地下一场雪
听雪落进时间的瓮中
朗诵给不可见的听众

有时礼物替我们说话
月亮高高地卡在天空上
爱在她废弃的花园里游
在无名小舟上飘飘荡荡
请尊重我的传统导向
微弱的火苗之上
来自拂晓的光

一把乌德琴，却无人弹唱
无数个词语沙粒里藏
承接你的种子和信仰
时隔多年又写一行
直到有一天，思绪如波浪
赞美女孩眼中的水光
幸福在分享中得到形状
旋律轻柔响起并给情绪定调
它为我生命中的每一刻奏响

This Poem Is Dedicated to Us
这首诗献给我们

This poem is jointly composed on the same topic.
The authors in turn are as follows:

此诗为同题联合创作，作者依次为：

Cida Pedrosa 西达·佩德罗萨

Rodrigo Luiz Pakulski Vianna 罗德里戈·维安纳

Nagat Ali 娜贾特·阿里

Ana Rüsche 安娜·鲁什

Alaa Hassan Fouda 阿拉·哈桑·福达

Júlia de Carvalho Hansen 朱莉娅·汉森

Ahmat Zakaria 艾哈迈德·扎卡里亚

方石英 Fang Shiying

Rawan Talal 拉万·塔拉勒

赵汗青 Zhao Hanqing

胡 桑 Hu Sang

刘 康 Liu Kang

Luiza Romão 路易莎·罗芒

Prithviraj Taur 普里特威拉杰·陶尔

Feben Fancho 费本·方乔

Kianoosh Khan Mohammadi 基亚努什·汉·穆罕默迪

Ivan Alekseev 伊万·阿列克谢耶夫

桑 子 Sang Zi

Hassan Amer 哈桑·阿米尔

Alfred Schaffer 阿尔弗雷德·萨弗尔

Amel Alsahlawi 阿迈勒·萨赫拉维

Elizaveta Kheresh 丽莎·赫列什

王二冬 Wang Erdong

Evgeniia Uliankina 叶芙根尼娅·乌里扬金娜

Sharif Al-Shafiey 谢里夫·沙菲伊

马骥文 Ma Jiwen

Mohammad Hossein Bahramian 穆罕默德·侯赛因·巴赫拉米扬

张小末 Zhang Xiaomo

Lubi Prates 卢比·普拉特斯

Mangaliso Buzani 曼加利索·布扎尼

Maksim Khatov 马克西姆·哈托夫

王单单 Wang Dandan

余 退 Yu Tui

冯 娜 Feng Na

Huda Almubarak 胡达·穆巴拉克

Vonani Bila 沃纳尼·比拉

Hatim Alshehri 哈特姆·谢赫里

熊 焱 Xiong Yan

Edrees Bakhtiari 伊德里斯·巴赫蒂亚里

Aditya Shukla 阿迪蒂亚·舒克拉

江 汀 Jiang Ting

Mxolisi Nyezwa 姆多利西·涅祖瓦

杨碧薇 Yang Biwei

Tsegaye Hailesilassie Girmay 策加耶·吉尔梅

Sultan Saud Alotaibi 苏尔坦·戴特

梁书正 Liang Shuzheng

Maksim Dremov 马克西姆·德廖莫夫

谈 骁 Tan Xiao

Hafez Azimi Kalkhuran 哈菲兹·阿齐米·卡尔胡兰

Viacheslav Glazyrin 维亚切斯拉夫·格拉济林

肖 水 Xiao Shui

张二棍 Zhang Ergun

Seife Temam 塞费·泰曼

戴潍娜 Dai Weina

李啸洋 Li Xiaoyang

Fatima Badr 法蒂玛·巴德尔

年微漾 Nian Weiyang

Alireza Ghazveh 阿里-礼萨·加兹韦赫

Ahmed Yamani 艾哈迈德·叶麦尼

Hassan Alnajjar 哈桑·纳贾尔

Enock Shishenge 伊诺克·希申格

Andrei Cherkasov 安德烈·切尔卡索夫

Thiago Ponce 蒂亚戈·庞塞

Shaikha Almteiri 谢哈·穆泰里

卢 山 Lu Shan

Feben Fancho 费本·方乔

Nikhilesh Mishra 尼基莱什·米什拉

Parvathy Salil 帕尔瓦缇·萨利尔

Mohamed Elmotayam 穆罕默德·穆塔亚姆

吕周杭 Lü Zhouhang

Gaireyah Fredericks 盖蕾娅·弗雷德里克斯

Gautam Vegda 高塔姆·维格达

国际
青春诗会
International Youth Poetry Festival

CONTENTS
目录

جوان

Молодость

青春 Youth

जवानी الشباب

Juventude

Brazil 巴西

ifigêniaa
伊菲革涅亚

路易莎·罗芒　诗人、演员、学者，圣保罗大学文学理论与比较文学在读博士。代表作有诗集《莫托洛夫的鸡尾酒》《血流成河》《我们这里也保存石头》。作品入选《当代 29 位诗人》等多部诗歌合辑。曾获 2022 年雅布提奖最佳诗集＆最佳图书奖等。此外，诗人还据她的著作创作了一些融合诗歌、电影和表演艺术的作品，她多次参加巴西、欧洲和拉美各个诗歌节。

Luiza Romão

路易莎·罗芒

Luiza Romão (b.1992) is a poet, actress and researcher. Academically, she is a PhD student in literary theory and comparative literature at the University of São Paulo. Her main works include poetry selections *Coquetel Motolove, Sangria, Também guardamos pedras aqui* and multimedia projects based on her poetry. Her poems are included in *29 poetas hoje* and other anthologies. She is the winner of the Jabuti Prize for Best Poetry Book and Best Book of 2022 and second place in Brazilian Poetry Slam Competition (SLAM BR) in 2014. She has participated in a lot of literary festivals in Europe and Latin America.

伊菲革涅亚 *

西方文学始于一场战争

而非城邦的迷雾

太久远了，或许我恍惚听闻

西方文学是从大屠杀肇始的

你呼吸它 犹如航海的人

目击一本永远摊开的书

现在轮到我来讲这段故事

这个契约只剩下石头

和沥青下的河流 这场雾霭

如今被唤作避难所

唇瓣上干枯的种子

在第一个字母之前

在第一个谜语之前

有人还乞求仁慈

而我已准备好谣曲

孩子们也需入眠

（黄茜 译）

---

* 伊菲革涅亚是《荷马史诗》中迈锡尼国王阿伽门农的长女。为了平息狩猎女神阿尔忒弥斯的愤怒，让军队得以出海，她被带到阿伽门农的军营里献祭。但在刀斧砍向她脖颈的瞬间，伊菲革涅亚消失无踪，一头公鹿取代了她的位置。

Ifigêniaa

literatura ocidental começou com uma Guerra

não a neblina das grandes cidades

faz tanto tempo que talvez ouço quase

a literatura ocidental começou com um massacre

isso você respira como quem veleja

o livro permanece aberto vê

é minha vez de contar a história

esse pacto só sobraram pedras

e rios sob o asfalto esse nevoeiro

agora chamam de santuário

o sêmen sobre os lábios seco

antes da primeira letra

antes do primeiro grifo

alguém já implorava misericórdia

estou pronta a canção

também as crianças precisam dormir

condição: imigrante (1)
条件: 他城之民 (选一)

卢比·普拉特斯　诗人、译者、编辑，圣保罗大学人类发展心理学博士。已出版 4 部作品，代表作有诗集《黑色的身体》《至今》。《黑色的身体》曾获得巴西 PROAC 诗歌创作发表扶持基金，入围第 4 届里约文学奖和第 61 届雅布提奖。翻译过美国女诗人玛雅·安吉罗、琼·乔丹等人的作品。曾参与组织巴西"我是诗人"女性诗歌节等活动，担任巴西海洋文学奖、雅布提文学奖等奖项的评委。有作品在阿根廷、哥伦比亚、克罗地亚、美国、法国、葡萄牙、瑞士翻译出版。

Lubi Prates
卢比·普拉特斯

Lubi Prates (b.1986) is a poet, translator, editor and literature curator. She has a PhD in human development psychology from the University of São Paulo (USP). She has published four books *coração na boca* (2012), *triz* (2016), *um corpo negro* (2018), *até aqui* (2021). Her book *um corpo negro*, awarded by PROAC with a grant for the creation and publication of poetry, was a finalist for the 4th Rio Literature Prize and the 61st Jabuti Prize. She has translated the works of many authors such as Maya Angelou, Audre Lorde and June Jordan. She was a judge for the Sesc Literature Prize, Oceanos Prize and Jabuti Prize. Her works have been translated and published in Argentina, Colombia, Croatia, United States, France, Portugal and Switzerland. She co-organized some literary festivals for the visibility of women poets, and also participated in literary festivals in Brazil and other countries in Latin America and Europe.

条件：他城之民（选一）

自从我来到这里
一条狗就一直跟着我

即使在我们之间
有几公里的距离
那障碍一重又一重

我仍能感觉到
它在我脖子上热乎乎的呼吸。

自从我来到这里
一条狗就一直跟着我

它不让我去时尚的地方
不让我使用与这里不同的方言
我把我的俚语
藏在行李箱的最底层
它狂吠着

自从我来到这里
一条狗就一直跟着我

我给它起了个绰号
叫"他城之民"。

（姚风 译）

condição: imigrante (1)

desde que cheguei
um cão me segue

&

mesmo que haja quilômetros
mesmo que haja obstáculos

entre nós

sinto seu hálito quente
no meu pescoço.

desde que cheguei
um cão me segue

&

não me deixa
frequentar os lugares badalados

não me deixa
usar um dialeto diferente do que há aqui
guardei minhas gírias no fundo da mala
ele rosna.

desde que cheguei
um cão me segue

&

esse cão, eu apelidei de
imigração.

"SE BEM QUE começasse azul"
"虽然以蓝为开端"

蒂亚戈·庞塞　诗人、译者，里约热内卢联邦学院教授。已出版多本诗集和散文集:《IMP》(2006),《懒散的姿态或没有姿态》(2010),《你向着光弯折》（2016，入围雅布提奖短名单），《一张照片》(2017),《坏疽》(2023)，及葡英双语作品集《光荣之盒》(2016,由英国诗人罗伯·帕克译介)。他还出版了散文集《桨与翻转》(2012),《现在……也许是我和某人：阅读保罗·策兰和里卡尔多·雷耶斯的独特体验》（2014）。他翻译过现当代欧洲、拉美和阿拉伯诗人的作品。多次参加国内国际文学活动。

Thiago Ponce
蒂亚戈·庞塞

Thiago Ponce (b.1986) is a Brazilian poet, translator and professor of Federal Institute of Rio de Janeiro. He is the author of the poetry collections *Imp.* (2006), *De gestos lassos ou nenhuns* (2010), *dobres sobre a luz* (2016), *uma fotografia* (2017), *Espacelamentos* (2023) and essay selection *Remos e Versões* (2012). His book *dobres sobre a luz* was shortlisted to the Jabuti Prize, the most important literary prize in Brazil. Participated in several national and international festivals, he translated the works of modern and contemporary poets from Latin America, Europe and the Arab world.

"虽然以蓝为开端"

虽然以蓝为开端

它随即变得更深

试图这样吸收风

和时代的浓重

从黑到白

光焰炽烈

让任何人的眼睛

永远向着

苍穹注视

自居间的

无法破解的

各种灰，到你眼里

斑驳的模糊色彩

每一次

太阳和云朵

在浩瀚混沌中

相互作用

随后纷纭的红诞生

"SE BEM QUE começasse azul"

SE BEM QUE começasse azul

e então se adensasse

tentando assim assimilar o vento

e o espesso do tempo

abrangendo desde o preto

até o branco numa intensidade

que fizesse qualquer um

fitar o firmamento

para sempre

desde os tons cinzentos

intermediários e tampouco

decifráveis até a cor vaga

que te parecesse vária

a cada vez que

sol e nuvens interagissem

nessa confusão de imenso

depois vermelhos que nascessem

e então os rosas que passasses

你转而钦慕玫瑰粉

相对于赤黄以及

金黄的诸色调

加倍为它泼洒的紫红

或非全部但可确信

生活的无从辨认的面庞

被夜之沥青

驱逐的印痕

（黄茜 译）

a admirar perante os púrpuras

a que se dobram gastos

os alaranjados e também

os matizes dourados

ou nem tanto mas sem dúvida

faces indiscerníveis da vida

traços dispersados

pelo breu da noite

2 de março
3月2日

朱莉娅·汉森 诗人，创意写作、文学、占星学教师。圣保罗大学文学学士，里斯本新大学葡萄牙语硕士。著有 5 本诗集，2016 年出版的《毒树液或果实》聚焦诗歌与植物关系，被归类为"蔬菜文学"，成为多所大学阅读、讨论的书籍。她经常参加各种研讨会、辩论会和文学活动，包括两次参加巴西帕拉蒂文学节（2018，2021）。曾担任 2019 年、2022 年、2023 年巴西海洋文学奖评委。她还是由女性编辑组成的独立出版公司"游乐场"的创始人之一。

Júlia de Carvalho Hansen
朱莉娅·汉森

Júlia de Carvalho Hansen (b.1984) is a poet, teacher of creative writing, literature and astrology. A literature graduate from the University of São Paulo, she has a Master's degree in Portuguese studies from the Universidade Nova de Lisboa. She's the author of five books including poetry selections *Romã* (Pomegranate) and *Seiva veneno ou fruto* (Sap Venom or Fruit), a book discussed in several universities and categorized as "vegetable literacy". She was a judge for one of the most important awards in Brazilian literature, the Oceanos Prize, in 2019, 2022 and 2023. She attended Festa Literária de Paraty, the most important literary event in Brazil, in 2018 and 2021.

3月2日

当人们彼此着迷

你喜欢上一个人

就会通过语义学

发明共同的语言 或者

水中的螺旋物

有些类似神奇的 DNA

它们围绕着你和对方

语言 (它属于我们

这样的物种) 绕来绕去

像一个无形而微妙的呼啦圈

在你的腰间旋转

让你的腰部颤抖

你被文字的魔力迷住了

很久之后, 过了很久之后

有时魔力会变成一粒种子

有时会变成一种流逝的仪式——一条河流

一连串从未有过的数字

门拍打着道路, 唤起

对未来或革命的恐惧

这也叫爱情。

(姚风 译)

2 de março

Quando a gente se encanta uma pessoa
pela outra a gente se encanta pela pessoa
e por uma semântica que vai sendo criada
em comum uma língua ou uma hélice
helicoidal bem úmida uma coisa meio
mágica meio DNA que fica girando
em torno de você e da outra pessoa
e que as palavras (por serem nossas,
da espécie) contornam e dão contorno
como um bambolê invisível e sútil
as palavras rodopiam vem pela cintura
dando uns arrepios no baixo da lombar
a gente se encanta pela mágica vocabular.
Aí passa muito tempo – e depois de muito tempo
às vezes a mágica virou uma semente
às vezes um rito de passagem – um rio
uma enumeração sem precedentes
a porta batendo a estrada chamando
o medo do depois ou a revolução
chamada também de amor.

"o movimento dos ombros"
"肩膀的运动引导飞行"

罗德里戈·维安纳　诗人、记者、教师。出版有诗集《让你记得去海滩的文字》《维阿那》《那不是一座城市》。曾获 2019 年马拉阿奖、2021 年巴西国家图书馆基金会颁发的阿方索斯·吉马良斯奖。

青春，如风有信

20

Rodrigo Luiz Pakulski Vianna
罗德里戈·维安纳

Rodrigo Luiz Pakulski Vianna (b.1981) is a poet, journalist and teacher. His representative works include poetry selections *Textos para Lembrar de Ir à Praia, Vianna and não era uma cidade*. He is the winner of the Maraã Prize in 2019 and Alphonsus Guimaraens Prize from the Fundação Biblioteca Nacional in 2021.

"肩膀的运动引导飞行"

你需要的动作在你的肩上

列侬 / 麦卡特尼

肩膀的运动引导飞行
改变方向
你需要打开胸膛

在鸟儿所有的勇敢行为中
它的歌声
就像它的存在一样简单

太阳在它的翅膀下破晓

利爪攫住了云

"o movimento dos ombros"

the movement you need
is on your shoulder
Lennon/McCartney

o movimento dos ombros
orienta o voo
para
alterar a rota é preciso
abrir o peito

----

de todas as coragens do pássaro
o seu canto
resulta
tão simples feito
o seu existir

sob seus pés o sol amanhece

as unhas nas nuvens

鸟群

杓鹬的短趾

撑起天空

鸟儿的道路
解体

如此急切，如出现时一样

我创作了以前的运动
以前的运动
我的写作是发生在翅膀上的
记忆
是对翅膀上发生的事情的记忆
是记忆翅膀上发生的事情

我看着过去在我眼前发生

----

revoada

os dedos curtos da
araucária só
seguram o céu

------

os caminhos das aves se desmancham

tão urgentes quanto aparecem

----

invento o movimento anterior
o momento anterior
a minha criação é a memória
do que acontece na asa
com o que aconteceu na asa
com o que aconteceu na asa
com o que aconteceu na asa

olho o passado acontecer
bem na minha frente

月亮没有了飞鸟

依旧允许星星闪烁

鸽子守护着
所有孤独的雕像

秋天的树
如时间的沙漏

黄叶飞舞
一片片

如鸟儿
张开翅膀

述说鸟儿即是在扼杀鸟儿
生命的一部分

a lua ausente
de pássaros se permitiu
as estrelas

----

as pombas guardam as estátuas de toda solidão

----

no outono a árvore
ampulheta

amarelo
caindo
voo
a voo

para expor as aves

----

dizer o pássaro já é matar
algo
que nele vive

即使明天它的翅膀会坠落

它的身体会腐烂

它的歌声会沉寂

它吃掉的那些昆虫不再维持

它的飞翔

比起大快朵颐的蛆虫

更可怕的是

在黄颜色的图画中描画鸟儿

笔下没有不朽

只有眼睛的瞬间

这个词只存在于过去

鸟儿从鸟儿身上被分割下来

叶子

　　蝴蝶

　　飘然落地

（姚风 译）

mesmo que amanhã suas asas

declinem sua carne escureça seu canto

silencie

e os insetos dos quais hoje

se alimenta festem-se do que o

mantinha em voo ainda

pior que os vermes em banquete

é dizer o pássaro em seu desenho amarelo

não há imortalidade na pena

há apenas o momento do olho

a palavra só existe em passado

corta do pássaro o pássaro

----

a folha é
   a borboleta
  até
    o pouso

imenso

庞 然

———

安娜·鲁什 诗人、小说家、学者，英语文学博士，圣保罗大学文学与气候危机专业博士后。2005 年出版处女作诗集《拉斯加达》（2008，西语版），此后继续出版有诗集《愤怒：纪念版》（2016；英译本，2017），西、葡双语《怪物》（2019）等 5 本诗集。她拍摄的记录片《我们热爱的我们》曾获得圣保罗文化厅 ProAC 资助（2010）。她还写有 3 本小说，最后一部《他人即通灵》是科幻小说，获得"奥迪塞亚奇幻文学奖"，并入围雅布提文学奖决选名单，该书已在意大利翻译出版。她多次参加国内国际文学活动，如纽约美洲诗歌节等。

Ana Rüsche
安娜·鲁什

Ana Rüsche (b.1979), a PhD in English literature, is currently conducting post-doctoral research on literature and climate crisis, University of Sao Paulo. She made her debut with the poetry selection *Rasgada* (2005), followed by four poetry selections including *Furiosa* and *Nós que Adoramos um Documentário* as well as science fiction novelette *A telepatia são os outros* (Telepathy Is Other People). She is the winner of Odisseia de Literatura Fantástica and ProAC of Secretaria da Cultura de São Paulo. Some of her works have been translated into Spanish, Italian and English. She has participated in literature festivals in Brazil and other countries, such as El Vertigo de Los Aires (Mexico), Poquita Fe (Chile) and The Americas Poetry Festival of New York.

庞 然

年龄跨度很大的孩子，长着翅膀和光环的摩托骑手，天堂
的护士，空荡荡的公交车的司机，值班的摄影记者，早起
的面包师，紫色头发的祖母，没有传记的诗人，忧伤的园
艺师的寡妇，邻居，每个人，

每个人
都在呼吸，呼吸
眼睛睁得大如茶杯，深如茶杯。
睁大布满血丝、充满睡意的眼睛，被外面的晨曦撕开的缝隙。

每个人
耳边依旧回响着龙吟
而肋骨上漫长的黑夜，

只为最终看见那个庞然大物。

它缓缓穿过我们的道路，如时间般黏稠，
它慢悠悠地走在我们的道路上，
它停下来。一日即将过去，我们继续前行。

（姚风 译）

imenso

crianças espichadas de idade, motoboys de asas e auréola,
enfermeiras celestes, motoristasde ônibus vazios,
fotojornalistas de plantão, padeiros madrugadores, avós
de cabelo roxo, poetas sem biografia, viúvas jardineiras da
tristeza, vizinhos, todo mundo,

todo mundo
respirando, respirando
com olhos tão largos e fundos quanto xícaras de chá.
tão largos e avermelhados de sono e sangue, rasgos de aurora
  lá fora.

todo mundo
ainda com bafo dos dragões dos ouvidos e
a noite tão longa das costelas, para,

finalmente ver a imensa criatura imensa.

a que cruza nosso caminho, lenta, gosmenta como os tempos
muito lenta, em nosso caminho, parada. um dia passará
  para que depois possamos prosseguir

fotografia de guerra
战争照片

西达·佩德罗萨　巴西共产党党员，诗人、小说家、伯南布哥州累西腓市议员。20 世纪 80 年代毕业于法律专业，同时参加了独立作家的运动，该运动汇集了边缘作家，经常举办朗诵会和街头表演、展览、图书集市，出版杂志和小册子，这一运动现已被公认为巴西文学史的一部分。诗人已出版 12 本诗集，代表作有《红金刚鹦鹉》、《莉莉丝的女儿们》等。她曾获得圣保罗艺术评论家协会 2022 年最佳诗集奖、2020 年雅布提年度诗集＆图书奖等。

Cida Pedrosa
西达·佩德罗萨

Cida Pedrosa (b.1963) is a poet, short story writer, reciter and Communist. Her representative works include *Araras Vermelhas* (Red Macaws), *Solo para Vialejo* (Solo for Vialejo), and *As filhas de Lilith* (The Daughters of Lilith). She has won Jabuti "Poetry" and "Book of the Year" (2020), APCA-Associação Paulista de Críticos de Artes "Best Poetry Book" (2022), Guerra Junqueiro Lusofonia Literary Prize 2023, etc.

战争照片

穿红衬衫和棕色小皮鞋的男孩
在冰冷的土耳其海边的沙滩上
伸展身体，化作文字
在我的诗中窒息而亡

穿粉色格子运动衫的女孩
用精美但残破的蝴蝶蒙住旧洋娃娃的眼睛
让她无法看到叙利亚地毯上的死者
文字浸染着恐惧
隐藏在我的诗行里

没有头发的孩子们瞳孔凸出
裸着身体，在索马里向游客
伸出没有血色的双手
这给我上了一堂艰难的解剖课
并为我的诗歌提供了饥饿一词

（姚风 译）

fotografia de guerra

o menino de camisa vermelha e sapatinhos
marrons estirado na areia do mar gélido da
Turquia migrou para a palavra e se afogou
no meu poema

a menina de moletom rosa-choque
desenhado com delicadas e surradas
borboletas tapando os olhos da boneca
esfarrapada impedindo a visão do tapete de
mortos no chão da Síria impregnou de medo
a palavra e se escondeu no meu poema

as crianças sem cabelo de pupilas
esbugalhadas e nuas estendendo as mãos
sem cor para os visitantes da Somália me
deram a mais difícil aula de anatomia e
ofertaram a palavra fome para o meu poema

جوان

Молодость

青春 Youth

الشباب जवानी

Juventude

Russia 俄罗斯

Из цикла «Формалисты». II.
组诗《形式主义者》之二

丽莎·赫列什 诗人、译者、学者，《旗帜》杂志编辑。现就读于俄罗斯高等经济大学语言学系。作品见于《词形》《夸脱》等杂志。曾任 2023 年马雅可夫斯基诗歌锦标赛评委。2023 年获安德烈·别雷奖。

Elizaveta Kheresh
丽莎·赫列什

Elizaveta Kheresh (Лиза Хереш, b.2002) is a poet, translator, literature researcher and editor of magazine *Flags*. She is studying at the Department of Philology of HSE University. She was the judge of Mayakovsky Poetry Championship (2023) and winner of Andrei Bely Prize of 2023.

组诗《形式主义者》之二

罗曼·雅各布森坐在布拉格一家咖啡馆里
喑哑的饼干掉在他膝盖上碎散开
一只膝盖
咖啡浮沫中
学生的脸孔与天使交替出现

听说
他不是雅各的儿子，而是雅各本人
他膝盖上的两种敲击相互对立
如同两种声音裂解开来，蟒蛇
也是如此将膝盖骨绕成一块飞地
好似在布拉格药店房顶生产的鸟

据说在旧俄时他每天夜里
都会单独同一位犹太老天使出去
他教他语音学，但却
不愿帮忙，只用火把将元音照亮

Из цикла «Формалисты». II.

роман якобсон сидит в пражском кафе
глухое печенье крошится на его колени
колено одно
лица учеников
чередуются с ангелами в кофейной пене

слышали
он не сын, он иаков сам
на его колене удары стоят в оппозиции
как два звука распадаются, так и удав
обвивает коленную чашу в анклав
как на пражской аптеке рожают птицы

говорят в старой россии он каждую ночь
выходил один на один со старым ангелом-
евреем, он учил его фонетике, и помочь
не хотел, только гласные освещал факелом

趁天还没黑

他打道回府

雅各布森不是雅各的儿子，他

是宙斯从一只膝盖中生下的

一瘸一拐地，上过战场

讲过《塔木德》经，就像槭树

在音位粗糙的舌头上磕磕绊绊

最后一次战斗时，空气清新

雅各布森失去了舌头

似乎还失去了儿子——因为战斗没有规则可言

依照家族习俗他也一向是用膝盖挟带着他

——因为在那之后众目睽睽之下

他垂下头

赢是赢了

但不怎么管事了

他似乎并不掩饰流产的伤痕

不过讲台后面本来也看不见

他坐上火车逃走

他更喜欢

廉价的半甜葡萄酒

засветло

уходил домой

якобсон не был сыном, он был рожден

зевсом через одно колено

заранее хромал выходя на бой

и толкуя через талмуд, как клен

спотыкается о шершавый язык фонемы

в последней драке воздух был чист

якобсон потерял в ней язык

и кажется сына, потому что бой велся без правил

тоже носил его в колене, как повелось в роду

потому что после того у всех на виду

он как поник

победил

мало правил

шрамы от выкидыша кажется не скрывал

но из-за кафедры не было видно

сбежал на поезде

предпочитал

дешевые и полусладкие вина

他曾像被延展成方糖那样地活着

介于有意义与无意义

二者之间

但对于老者和其他迎面走来的人

他膝盖上的伤疤却清晰可见

罗曼·雅各布森

据说

并不怀念旧俄罗斯

他也不记得语言

只要是有面包吃

有谢谢说

但学生们听说

在西伯利亚

仍有天使继续, 跪下来

继续向杂语

传授爱

（刘高辰 译，易宁 编校）

жил, как вытянутый в сахарный куб

положен был между означающим

и не очень

но его шрамы на колене видны

встречающим старикам и прочим

роман якобсон

говорят

не скучает по старой россии

он не помнит язык

только б в хлебе

или спасибе

но студенты слышали

что в сибири

продолжаются ангелы на колени вставать

и учить любви

гетероглоссии

БИТВА ЗА ХОГВАРТС
霍格沃茨之战

马克西姆·哈托夫 诗人，杂志《Translit》诗歌实验室学员。曾在线上刊物《中间色调》和《缺陷》上发表作品。

Maksim Khatov
马克西姆·哈托夫

Maksim Khatov (Максим Хатов, b.2002) is working in poetry magazine "TRANSLIT" laboratory. His poems were published on many online magazines.

霍格沃茨之战

你好，我是来自紫线躺在康复所的

绿发小子，你曾经的敌人
现在虽非
好友，但也算得上是个

熟人，你也好啊，你这不
再画

布尔什维克 CP 的、曾几何时
和我同去陵墓（或是
其他这种地方）
约会的小丫头，您也

好啊，维欣诺站幽灵般的

逻辑学家，涂鸦的长椅，不解地点头的
年轻人们，我再次呼吁你们所有人

守护城堡的废墟

（摘自《哈利·波特与吝啬的冤魂之花 II》组诗）

（刘高辰 译，易宁 编校）

БИТВА ЗА ХОГВАРТС

привет тебе лежащий в рехабе зеленоволосый паренек с

фиолетовой ветки бывший враг
теперь не
то что бы друг но в целом хороший

знакомый привет и тебе больше
не рисующая

пэйринги большевиков девчонка с которой мы
когда-то ходили в мавзолей на
свидание (или

что-то вроде того) привет и

вам тоже станция выхино призрачные

логики крашеные скамейки недоуменно кивающие
юнцы я снова призвал вас всех чтобы

защищать развалины замка

(ИЗ ЦИКЛА «ГАРРИ ПОТТЕР И СКУПЫЕ ЦВЕТЫ НЕДОЖИВШИХ II»)

первая трава
最初的草地

马克西姆·德廖莫夫　诗人，俄罗斯高等经济大学俄罗斯文学及比较文学研究硕士。2017 年开始发表诗歌，2020 年出版诗集《月、水、草》。作品见于《空气》《新文学视野》等刊物。2021 年入围德拉戈莫申科诗歌奖决选名单，获《蝉》诗歌奖。有作品译为英文及波兰文。

Maksim Dremov
马克西姆·德廖莫夫

Maksim Dremov (Максим Дремов, b.1999) earned his Master's degree in Russian literature and comparative literature studies from HSE University. Since 2017, his poems have been published in major Russian magazines. His poetry selection *Moon Water Grass* was published in 2020. Shortlisted for Arkady Dragomoshchenko Prize in 2021, he won Cicada Award in 2021. Some of his poems have been translated into English and Polish.

最初的草地

今天，在城市里还有什么能做的，
且来看看草地：

看看你在的时候，
姑娘们透过栅栏指指点点，

哄笑的地方；当你躺着时，露水——
是巫师的占卜球；膝盖——

是触感的传送门，
传送到塔兰图拉毒蛛的洞穴遍布城市的时代，

超心理学的经验：名字
从树叶上落下，装着草的袋子

阳光倾泻，记录着
孩童大胆的触碰；看——

有如对草的守望：看着它
直接在眼前发芽长大；

触碰——就像太阳
从你的影子里跳开时那样。

（摘自《草》组诗）

（李昀庆、易宁 译）

первая трава

что вообще делать сегодня в городе,
кроме как смотреть на траву:

смотреть, пока бываешь там, где
девушки тычут пальцем сквозь решётку

со смехом; когда лежишь, роса —
это гадательный шар; колено —

тактильный портал во времена,
когда в городе зияли норы тарантулов,

парапсихотический опыт: имя,
упавшее из листвы, мешки с травой,

солнечный оползень, снимающий
детскую наглость касания; смотреть —

это как дожидаться травы: пока она
прорастёт прямо через глаза;

касаться — это как солнце в тот самый
момент, когда оно отпрыгнуло от твоей тени.

(Из цикла «Трава»)

"щепотка лазоревой соли"
"一小撮蔚蓝色的盐"

伊万·阿列克谢耶夫 中文名"易宁"，诗人、诗歌学者。乌拉尔联邦大学东方学学士、世界文学硕士，北京师范大学文学院在读博士，师从张清华教授，研究方向为中国现当代文学、中国当代诗歌。2013年始习诗，2018年开始翻译，译著包括《火焰内部：海子的诗》《西川诗选》（待出版）等。现居北京。

Ivan Alekseev
伊万·阿列克谢耶夫

Ivan Alekseev (Иван Алексеев, b.1994) primarily regards himself as a poetry translator with some occasional original contributions to the poetry field. He graduated from Ural Federal University (BA: Asian and African studies; MA: world literature) and now is doing his PhD in contemporary Chinese literature under the supervision of Prof. Zhang Qinghua. Ivan dates his first poetic and translation drafts back to 2013 and 2018 respectively. His significant publications include *Inside the Flames: Poetry by Hai Zi* (2021) and *Starring: Me. Selected Poems by Xi Chuan* (exp. 2024). Currently he lives in Beijing.

"一小撮蔚蓝色的盐"

一小撮蔚蓝色的盐
沸腾的广场。车站
你皱一皱眉吧，哪怕是因为疼痛
就那样做吧（若曾如此）

这动荡时日
自由迈出一小步
在触及天际之前
像根小草回到掌中

疾如被穿透的
辽远，被喧嚣掩映
请允许我在这里稍坐
现在我将允许你做一切

（吴婵艳 译）

"щепотка лазоревой соли"

щепотка лазоревой соли
кипящая площадь. вокзал
поморщься хотя бы от боли
бывай (если прежде бывал)

такое уж шаткое время
свободы шажок приставной
дотронувшись прежде до неба
травинка вернется в ладонь

на скорость как будто прошитый
простор, затушеванный в шум
я тут посижу, разрешите
сейчас я вам все разрешу

"Предчувствуя дождь..."
"预知到雨的来临……"

维亚切斯拉夫·格拉济林　诗人，乌拉尔联邦大学在读博士生、语言学院高级讲师，诗歌媒体"非现代人"的联合创始人和编辑。诗作发表在《拉之子》和《乌拉尔》杂志上。

Viacheslav Glazyrin
维亚切斯拉夫·格拉济林

Viacheslav Glazyrin (Вячеслав Глазырин, b.1994) is a senior lecturer and doctoral candidate of Ural Federal University, teaching linguistics at the Department of Philology for more than five years. He is the co-founder and editor of poetry media *Non-contemporary*. His poems were frequently published in the literary magazines *Ural* and *Children of Ra*.

"预知到雨的来临……"

1
预知到雨的来临，你醒了。
风摇动树木。
梦的轮廓
创作黑暗的血流。

为温暖寻名时，请你回忆：
妈妈唱着春天的歌曲。
被遗忘的梦境中的穹顶
如此之高。

2
雅各的梯子。
梦境的穹顶。
轻夏的失神。
父亲的侧脸。

从火焰深渊
我眼见一阵风，
群星
投射目光。

深红的金子。
雅各的梯子。
眼睛在说话。
梦继续生长。

（易宁、杨茂源、刘华正 译）

"Предчувствуя дождь..."

1
Ты проснёшься, предчувствуя дождь.
Ветер деревья качает.
Очертания сна
тьмы кровоток сотворят.

Нарекая тепло, вспоминай:
мама поёт о весне.
Своды забытого сна
высоки.

2
Иакова лествица.
Своды высокие сна.
Обморок лёгкого лета.
Профиль отца.

Из бездны огня
я ветер увижу,
созвездья развяжут
взгляд.

Багряное золото.
Иакова лествица.
Глаза говорят.
И сон продолжает расти.

"Если что говори как есть"
"若有什么便直说"

叶芙根尼娅·乌里扬金娜　诗人，2015 年毕业于莫斯科国立大学，社交媒体"电报"频道《头等诗人》节目主理人。诗歌发表在《汽船》《夸脱》等杂志和《中间色调》等门户网站上。已发表诗集《如生》。曾获"中学奖"第二名、"莫斯科帐户"小奖。

青春，如风有信

Evgeniia Uliankina

叶芙根尼娅·乌里扬金娜

Evgeniia Uliankina (Евгения Ульянкина, b.1992) is an editor of "Palindrome" digital agency. Graduated from Moscow State University in 2015, she was successively the owner of the channel "Essential Poetry" in Telegram, co-editor of the poetry section of the online literary magazine *Formasloff* and the poetry Telegram channel "Metajournal". She has published the poetry selection *As If Alive*. Her poems were published in different offline and online literary magazines including *Literratura*. She is the laureate of "Lyceum" (second prize for poetry, 2020) and "Moskovsky Schet" for the best debut book of 2021.

"若有什么便直说"

若有什么便直说

水升云浮

有生的万物终将散尽

悲伤是成年人的艺术

委曲求全无法避免

死亡来得不计其数

总之此时无可奈何

唯有静观

（杨茂源 译，易宁 编校）

"Если что говори как есть"

Если что говори как есть
Облако водяная взвесь
Всё рассыпется что росло
Горе взрослое ремесло
Необходимая кривизна
смерть приходит ей нет числа
в общем нечего тут уметь
только смотреть

"что я могу?"
"我能做什么？"

安德烈·切尔卡索夫　诗人。2012 年毕业于高尔基文学院，现就职于新文学视野出版社。出版有诗集《比想象更简单》《家务百科——双栏精选》《被分割的风》《失控情况》《备用边缘》等。他是 2016 年"普希金实验室"诗歌节森林奖得主，曾入围俄罗斯格列佛奖、安德烈·别雷奖和元杂志奖短名单。

Andrei Cherkasov
安德烈·切尔卡索夫

Andrei Cherkasov (Андрей Черкасов, b.1987) graduated from Maxim Gorky Literature Institute (creative writing, poetry) in 2012. He is the art manager of New Literary Observer Publishing House. His published poetry collections include *Easier than It Seems*, *Decentralized Observation, Circumstances Out of Control, Household-Selected from Two Columns, Wind by Parts*, etc. He is shortlisted for Russian Gulliver Prize (2014), Andrey Belyi Prize (2015, 2019), Metajournal Prize (2021) and winner of Pushkin Lab Festival Forest Prize (2016).

"我能做什么？"

我能做什么？

在任何
一天

行走在

微弱的火苗
之上

在寡淡的
共情
之中

在痛处
之上

在这一年
在这座城市里

在这一月

在这一年

再问一遍

我能做些什么？

（易宁、刘华正 译）

"что я могу?"

что я могу?

в любой
день

идти

над слабым
огнём

в слабом
растворе
солидарности

по слабым
местам

в этом году
в этом городе

в этом месяце

в этом году

ещё раз

что я могу?

جوان
Молодость
青春 Youth
जवानी الشباب
Juventude

Messengers
from the Vernal Wood

青春
如风有信

India 印度

It Rained Again
又下雨了

帕尔瓦缇·萨利尔 诗人。英国提赛德大学在读博士生。著有诗集《狂想曲》《我不认识的人》。曾受邀主持伦敦大学伯贝克学院伦敦批判理论暑期学校课程，并发起《诗意见证》课程。曾为全印广播电台的"青年之声"栏目朗诵诗歌，十余年来担任多场印度文学文化活动主持人。

青春，如风有信

Parvathy Salil
帕尔瓦缇·萨利尔

Parvathy Salil (b.1997) is currently a full-time PhD student in Teesside University, UK. She has authored two poetry collections, *Rhapsody* (2016) and *The One I Never Knew* (2018). As a guest participant invited to moderate group work sessions at the London Critical Theory Summer School at Birkbeck, University of London, she ideated and conducted "Poetic Witnessing", which has now been declared an official program of the summer school. She has recited poems for the All-India Radio's Yuvavani and has been hosting/moderating literary and cultural events in India for over a decade.

又下雨了

又下雨了，
此前，我独自站在灰色的沙粒上——
面对干燥、干枯、死亡。

清新的雾气之吻，
雨滴的芬芳
立刻抹去了干燥，很快
使其变得湿润、舒缓

我的脚轻抚雾蒙蒙的沙滩，
此刻，幸福的花蕾在我心中跳跃
我出神凝视
渴望它永不停止……

（颜海峰 译）

It Rained Again

It rained again,
As I stood alone on the grey sand grains —
Arid, dry and dead.

The fresh kiss of mist,
The fragrance of the drops
Erased at once the dryness, soon
Soothed, transformed it moist.

The misty sands, my feet caressed
As blossoms of bliss once bounced in me
I gazed, I gazed
Desiring if it never ceased...

Poetry

诗 歌

尼基莱什·米什拉 奥里亚语诗人、独立电影制作人，加尔各答萨蒂亚吉特·雷电影电视学院导演和剧本写作专业在读研究生。已出版诗集《某人某地》《诗人死后》和非虚构作品《原谅痛苦》。曾获小说新人奖、塔帕西亚基金会桑巴巴纳奖、阿纳米卡博士诗歌奖等。2020—2023 年间 5 次入选印度文学院青年文学奖短名单。

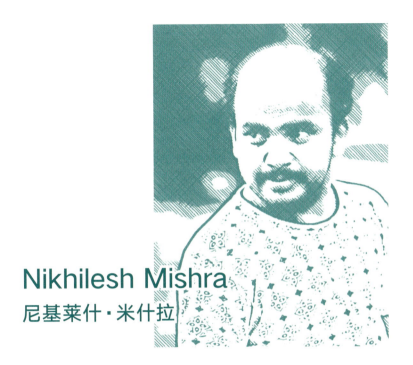

Nikhilesh Mishra
尼基莱什·米什拉

Nikhilesh Mishra (b.1996) is an independent filmmaker, an Odia poet and a postgraduate student of India Satyajit Ray Film and Television Institute. He has published poetry collections *Someone Somewhere, After A Poet Dies* and non-fiction *Forgive If It Hurt*. He is the laureate of KATHA Nabapratibha Prize, Tapasya Foundation Sambhabana Prize, Dr Anamika Poetry Prize, etc. And he was shortlisted for the SAHITYA AKADEMI YUVA PURASKAR five times in 2020-2023.

诗 歌

时隔多年又写了一行

当我看了一眼，
我大笑不止。
因为，感觉就像是
我从某个其他诗人的
想象中
摘取了这一行。

我不断尝试，却认不出
在那行诗中哭泣的孩子。
"你叫什么名字，宝贝？"
"你的妈妈在哪里？"
孩子不停地哭泣，伤心欲绝。

谢天谢地！在那一行中
有一个二十二岁的女孩。

Poetry

Wrote a line after ages

And laughed really hard
When I looked at it.
For, it felt like
I have just lifted this line
Off some other poet's
Imagination.

I kept trying but couldn't recognize
The child who was crying in that line.
'What's your name baba?'
'Where's your Ma?'
The child kept crying, bitterly.

Thank God! There was a
Twenty-two-year-old girl in that line.

她离家出走
到达了那里。她是
安慰那孩子的人。

但是，尽管那个女孩
看起来和我过去爱过的女孩一模一样，
却没有认出我。

我坐在那里，沉默地
和那一行诗在一起，
过了一段时间。
然后，我把那张纸
藏在一本旧小说里的
最后几页……

……就像我上次做的那样

（颜海峰 译）

She had run away from home
And had arrived there. She was
The one who consoled the child.

But the girl, though she looked
Exactly like the girl I used to be in love with,
Didn't recognize me.

I sat there in silence
With that line,
For some time.
And then, I hid that piece of paper
Inside an old novel,
Towards the last pages...

... like I had done the last time

The Cicada
蝉

高塔姆·维格达　用英语写作的达利特诗人、插画家、学者。古吉拉特邦中央大学博士生。著有诗集《秃鹰和其他诗歌》《血肉与骨头的奇怪案例》。作品被收录进《疯狂：世界诗歌选集》等。其作品主要聚焦于种姓压迫以及达利特人和妇女遭受的暴行。

Gautam Vegda
高塔姆·维格达

Gautam Vegda (b.1994), a PhD student in Central University of Gujarat, is a Dalit writer who writes in English and an illustrator. His main works include poetry collections *Vultures and Other Poems* (2018) and *A Strange Case of Flesh and Bones* (2019). He has contributed to several global anthologies such as *Madness: An Anthology of World Poetry* (2023). Gautam Vegda largely writes around the caste oppression and atrocities inflicted upon the Dalits and women.

蝉

我本不会赤着脚

在尘土飞扬的路上跋涉那么远，

我本不会辛勤工作

年复一年地气喘吁吁，

我本不会默默忍受

噩梦的暴戾，

如果没有音乐的陪伴，

但我从哪儿弄来一根琴弦？

我的音乐只不过是蝉鸣，

它为我生命中的每一刻演奏

从未让我体验到

在不可触碰的沙漠中

踽踽独行的经历

现在，当我阅读、写作和发言时，

蝉必定在发出旋律，

只要抵抗持续，

蝉就会继续以尖叫、噤声

滴血和炽热的纸张

同步抗议

我的斗争和蝉一样古老。

（颜海峰 译）

The Cicada

I couldn't have trudged barefooted
This far on the dusty road,
I couldn't have worked hard
Wheezily for years and years,
I couldn't have swallowed the ferocity
Of nightmares in utter silence,
Had I not been accompanied by music,
But where did I have even a single string?
My music was just the Cicada,
Never made me realize of the experience
Of walking alone in the desert
Of untouchability by serving music
To every moment of my existence.
Now, while I read, write and enunciate,
The Cicada must be leaking melodies,
As long as the resistance persists,
The Cicada will continue to sync
With screams, choke ups,
Dripping blood and fiery papers.
My struggle is as old as the Cicada.

मेरे गाँव में एक भी क़ब्र नहीं है
我的村里一座坟墓也没有

阿迪蒂亚·舒克拉 印地语诗人、小说家，保险信息公司质量分析师。
已出版诗集《若我把七大洋化作墨水》和系列小说《死亡三部曲》
《公寓三部曲》等，并发表诸多书评、影评。翻译过费尔南多·佩
索阿、罗贝托·波拉尼奥、弗兰兹·卡夫卡等人的作品。

Aditya Shukla
阿迪蒂亚·舒克拉

Aditya Shukla (b.1991) is a quality analyst of Illumifin India Pvt Limited. As a Hindi poet and fictionist, he has published poetry selections *Saat Samand ki Masi Karu* and short stories trilogies *Death Trilogy*, *Apartment Trilogy* as well as reviews on books and films. He translated the works of Roberto Bolano, Franz Kafka, Fernando Pessoa, etc.

我的村里一座坟墓也没有

我的村里，一座坟墓也没有，
但却有，很多很多的空地，
杂草，
砖瓦石块，水泥，还有干活的人。

人总是要死的，
而我的村里
有很多的花园。
我有自己的花园，
有自己的花草和绿植。

假如，我也拥有一个属于自己的坟墓……
沐浴在开阔的天空之下，
无论在哪里，
只要在上面刻上我的介绍，
我说过的话，
我做过的梦，
还有那，我一次又一次的挫败……
我把自己所有的花，一朵一朵地献于墓前。

如此，风花雪月便也从头上卸了下来。

（戈富平 译）

मेरे गाँव में एक भी क़ब्र नहीं है

मेरे गाँव में एक भी क़ब्र नहीं है,
लेकिन ख़ूब खुली-खुली जगहें हैं,
घास है,
ईंट-पत्थर-सीमेंट और कामगार हैं।

लोग मरते भी हैं बहुधा
मेरे गाँव में
फूल के बाग़ीचे हैं।
मेरे अपने बाग़ीचे,
मेरे अपने फूल-पौधे।

काश! मेरी अपनी एक क़ब्र भी होती–
खुले आसमान के नीचे,
कहीं भी,
जिस पर अंकित होता मेरा परिचय,
मेरे शब्द,
मेरे स्वप्न,
मेरी असफलताएँ...
एक-एक कर अपने सारे फूल मैं उस क़ब्र पर चढ़ा आता।

यूँ फूलों का बोझ मेरे सिर से उतर जाता।

Living Turned to Burning
活着变成了燃烧

普里特威拉杰·陶尔　马拉地语诗人、翻译家、评论家。斯瓦米·拉马南德·蒂尔特马拉瓦达大学马拉地语系主任、副教授，美术与表演艺术学院院长，马哈拉施特拉邦政府马拉地语咨询委员会成员、马哈拉施特拉邦地名词典部编辑委员会成员。他已出版著作 30 余种，诗集收录进新德里中央梵语大学的教学大纲。翻译过多部诗集和儿童文学作品，包括中国童话《小马过河》《骄傲的小花猫》等。

Prithviraj Taur
普里特威拉杰·陶尔

Prithviraj Taur (b.1979) is a Marathi poet, translator and critic. As Head & Associate Professor of Marathi Literature and Director of School of Fine and Performing Arts, Swami Ramanand Teerth Marathwada University, he is State Secretary of Sahitya Bharati, a member of the Editorial Board of the Maharashtra State Gazetteer Department and that of Marathi Language Advisory Board of the Maharashtra Government. He has more than 30 books to his credit and translated many poetry books and fairy tales including Chinese stories *Little Horse Crossed the River, Golden Bird and Cat.*

活着变成了燃烧

夜晚就这样过去:
燃烧的火焰在黑暗中熄灭。
生活瞬间化为
尘土。

我没有咬过任何人一口
也没有砍断任何人的翅膀。
而生活对我来说, 依然堕入赤贫
破败不堪。

活着变成了燃烧?
谁剪断了脐带?
可怕的死亡在日头下
淫逸骄奢。

（颜海峰 译）

Living Turned to Burning

The nights pass thus:
The burning flames extinguish in the dark.
And life's reduced to the dust
in a moment.

I didn't give anybody a bite
nor did I cut off anybody's wings.
Yet life for me is reduced to penury,
ruined.

Living turned into burning?
Who cut off the umbilical cord?
Pampered is the dreadful death
in the sun.

جوان

Молодость

青春 Youth

الشباب जवानी

Juventude

South Africa 南非

Inside the River
河中央

曼加利索·布扎尼　诗人，罗德斯大学创意写作硕士、教师。用英语、科萨语创作。他的第一部用科萨语写成的诗集《我还在写诗》(2014) 获得了 2015 年南非文学奖诗歌奖。《一根裸露的骨头》(2019) 是他的第一本英文诗集，获得了 2019 年格伦纳·卢谢伊非洲诗歌奖。

Mangaliso Buzani
曼加利索·布扎尼

Mangaliso Buzani (b.1978) is a teacher of creative writing at Rhodes University with a Master's degree in creative writing. His first collection *Ndisabhala Imibongo* (Imbizo Arts, 2014) written in isiXhosa, won the 2015 SALA Award for Poetry. *A Naked Bone* (Deep South, 2019) was his first book in English which won the 2019 Glenna Luschei Prize for African Poetry.

河中央

在河水中央
我想成为一条海狗
但我鼻子闻不出
河神的气味

在河水源头
我想成为一名作家
但这河水
无法让纸张保持干燥

在河的鞋子里
我想像基督一样行走
但河床
无法承受我双脚的重量

而我沉下去
给青蛙
读诗

（范静哗 译）

Inside the River

Inside the heart of the river
I want to be a sea-dog
but this nose can't sniff
the scent of umamlambo

inside the head of the river
I want to be a writer
but this water
can't keep the paper dry

inside the shoes of the river
I want to walk like christ
but the floor of the river
can't keep up the weight of my feet

and I sink
to read poems
to frogs

Don't Play with Your Heart
不要玩弄你的心

伊诺克·希申格　诗人，中学教师。2005 年开始创作，著有诗集《我的福音经文》《禁闭》《属于泪水和恐惧的时代》，自传《一个黑人孩子的挣扎》等。曾获非洲荣誉作家奖、南非民主教师联盟故事奖、OR 坦博世纪写作比赛奖、教育之星奖、OR 坦博散文写作奖等荣誉。

Enock Shishenge

伊诺克·希申格

Enock Shishenge (b.1977) serves as a teacher of Eqinisweni Secondary School, and writes from 2005. His main works include poetry selctions *Nsati wa gayisa*, *My Gospel Scriptures*, *Lockdown*, *Times of Tears and Fears*, novel *Muhloti wa tinyarhi…* and biography *Struggle of a Black Child*. He is the laureate of African Honoree Award for Poetry (2020, 2021), Sadtu Story Telling Award (2018), OR Tambo Centenary Writing Competition (2017), Star in Education Award, (2013) and OR Tambo Essay Writing (2010).

不要玩弄你的心

听着, 孩子, 让我告诉你一件事:
别以为我在开玩笑, 这是真的,
不要拿走你的心去玩弄它, 孩子;
把它交给诗人。

这些人是不一样的人;
他们的话是多愁善感的;
他们会让你允许他们拿走你的心;
他们不是人, 这些人。我亲眼见过他们。

听着, 孩子, 让我告诉你: 他们的话像糖一样甜。
他们偷偷劫走了玛丽亚, 让她生了个孩子
并欺骗约瑟说儿子来自圣灵
没有圣灵, 他们就是圣灵
他们是圣灵, 这些诗人
别相信诗人

我的孩子, 你可以问亚当叔叔, 他会告诉你真相
诗人给了夏娃禁果, 并谎称是蛇给她的
没有蛇, 那蛇就是诗人。

（赵四 译）

Don't Play with Your Heart

Listen child, let me tell you something:
Don't think I am joking this is true,
Don't take your heart and play with it child;
And give it to the poet.

These people are not people;
Their words are sentimental;
They will make you allow them to remove your heart;
They are not human these people.
I have seen them with my eyes.

Listen child, let me tell you: their words are so sweet like sugar.
They robbed Mariah and gave her a child in secret
And lied to Joseph that the son comes from the Holy Spirit
There was no Holy Spirit they were the Holy Spirit
They are the Holy Spirit these poets
Don't trust the poets

My child you can ask uncle Adam he will tell you the truth
The poet gave Evah the forbidden fruit and lied that she was
  given by the snake
There was no snake, the snake was the poet.

The African Woman
非洲女人

盖蕾娅·弗雷德里克斯　诗人。罗德斯大学创意写作硕士。著有诗集《开普语是荷兰语》《回声》《已经一分钟了》《斋月纪事》等，多次参加文学节并朗诵诗歌。曾获 2016 年麦克格雷戈尔帕特里夏·舍恩斯坦诗歌奖、2018 年开普语推广荣誉奖、内维尔·亚历山大威望奖、休·霍金斯在场奖等奖项。

Gaireyah Fredericks
盖蕾娅·弗雷德里克斯

Gaireyah Fredericks (b.1977) got her Master's Degree of Arts in creative writing from Rhodes University. She is the author of poetry books *Kaaps Is Hollands*, *Echoes*, *It's Been a Minute*, *Ramadan Chronicles* and so on. She won the "2016 Patricia Schonstein Poetry in McGregor" Award, Promotion of Kaaps Honorary Award 2018, Neville Alexander Prestige Award, Hugh Hodgens "on the spot" Award (2022, 2023), etc.

非洲女人

在这非洲的阳光下，越过非洲的平原，

山山水水之上，孕育着辉煌和伟大的创造。

她，一个头脑简朴的生灵，有多种色调、不同颜色，能说多种语言。

她的心随着他们古老的鼓声而跳动，保持着习俗和文化的节拍。

她赤脚走在人生的石子路上，

将她所爱之人的重负完美地顶在头上。

她洗刷了误会和远远不够的欣赏，

以瀑布源源流出的水晶般清澈的水。

她用葱郁的绿色象叶遮盖自己的贞洁，并将脸涂成白色。

她抬起下巴，站在期待已久的雨中，

要浇灭过去的压迫所带来的干燥心态。

她是谁？

她是自由、解放与独立的子宫。

她是一位非洲女人。

（范静哗 译）

The African Woman

Under this African sun, beyond the African planes and

over rivers and mountains, lies creation of magnificence and
grandeur.

A simple minded being with many shades, diverse colors and
she speaks in many tongues.

Her heart beats to their ancient drums, keeping the beat with
customs and culture.

She walks bare feet on the gravel roads of life and

carries her loved one's burdens beautifully balanced on her head.

She washes the misunderstandings and under appreciation

in the crystal-clear waters flowing steadily from the waterfalls.

She covers her chastity in the lush green elephant leaves and
paints her face white.

She lifts her chin and basks in the long-awaited rain to
quench

the dry mentality of passed oppression.

Who is she?

She's the womb of freedom, liberty and independence.

She is an African woman.

Day(dream) # 207
白日（梦）（第 207 号）

阿尔弗雷德·萨弗尔　南非语和荷兰语诗人、翻译家、《荷兰周报》文学评论员，现任斯坦陵布什大学阿非利卡语和荷兰语系高级讲师。已出版 10 本诗集，包括《我是谁。处罚规定》《人兽事》《笼子》《水沫》等。曾获约·彼得斯奖、许格斯·佩尔纳特奖、扬·坎珀特奖、夏洛特·科勒奖，以及胡夫特奖等。2021 年他凭迄今的全部作品赢得荷兰最具盛名的文学奖彼得·科尼利祖·霍夫特奖。

Alfred Schaffer
阿尔弗雷德·萨弗尔

Alfred Schaffer (b.1973) is an Afrikaans and Dutch poet, translator and senior lecturer at University of Stellenbosch, South Africa. He is also a literary reviewer for a Dutch weekly paper, *De Groene Amsterdammer*. He is the author of 10 poetry collections including *wie was ik. strafregels* (who was I. penalty rules, 2020), *Mens dier ding* (Man Animal Thing, 2014), *Kooi* (Cage, 2008), *Schuim* (Foam, 2006). He won Jo Peters Poetry Prize for his first collection, Hugues C. Pernath Prize, Ida Gerhardt Poetry Prize, Jan Campert Prize, Awater Poetry Prize, Paul Snoek Prize, Charlotte Köhler Prize, Herman de Coninck-Prize and the P.C. Hooft Prize 2021, the most prestigious literary prize in the Netherlands for an oeuvre.

白日（梦）（第 207 号）

当我回想起城市和所有那些水，正是夜间。

我站在街上，说不出是在哪里。

我必须回家所以抱着乐观态度跟着运河走。

正当我想着差不多到了

一只羚羊，害怕地喷着鼻息，

穿过黑色的水跑了过来。

三只鬣狗追逐着它，像只警报器

光的喷泉迸裂在它们脚下。

过了桥后自然灾难左拐

离开了视线，而后安静下来。白日里

这水没有臭味，船从中间滑行穿过

满载着挥手的游客，他们向骑自行车的人

向任何移动的东西，向那边那个男人挥手

那个男人想要飞走，似乎

胳膊伸展，被阴影笼罩

一只惊慌失措的受伤的鸟——不可能是巧合

那男人是我，不过我在狂乱地拍动翅膀

只是我没有离开地面。

而这时我真的想要回家了。

一定是在这里某处，我简直不能相信

在一片漆黑中我之所见。

（赵四 译）

Day(dream) # 207

When I think back to the city with all that water it's night-time.

I'm standing on the street I can't say where.

I have to go home so I follow the canal hoping for the best.

Just as I'm thinking I'm almost there

a gazelle, snorting with fear,

comes running across the black water.

Three hyenas are chasing it like an alarm

fountains of light bursting under their feet.

The natural disaster turns left after the bridge

out of sight and then it's quiet. In the daytime

this water doesn't stink, boats glide through the center

filled with tourists who wave at cyclists

and at everything that moves, at that man over there

who wants to fly away, it seems

arms spread, darkened by shadows

a wounded bird in panic – it cannot be coincidence

that the man is me, however frantically I flap

I just don't leave the ground.

And by now I really do want to go home.

It must be somewhere here, I can hardly believe

what I saw in the pitch dark.

Mandela, Have You Ever Wondered?
曼德拉，你有没有想过？

沃纳尼·比拉　聪加语及英语诗人，林波波大学英语讲师，诗歌杂志《缇姆比拉》创始人、编辑，"缇姆比拉图书"出版人，维姆贝国际诗歌节主任，"缇姆比拉作家之家"创始人，南非金山大学创意写作在读博士。著有英语、北索托语、聪加语创作的 8 本故事书，两本童书。他的主要作品包括诗集《以阿曼德拉之名》《魔力斯坦国的火》《俊美的吉塔》等。曾获 2012 年、2013 年索·普拉阿杰欧盟诗歌奖二等奖。

Vonani Bila
沃纳尼·比拉

Vonani Bila (b.1972) is a poet writing in Xitsonga and English. As a cultural activist, he is the founding editor of *Timbila* poetry journal, publisher of Timbila Books, curator of the Vhembe International Poetry Festival and founder of Timbila Writers' Village, a rural retreat center for writers. As a lecturer in English at the University of Limpopo, he is currently studying for a PhD (creative writing) at Wits University. He is the author of eight storybooks in English, Northern Sotho and Xitsonga for newly literate adult readers, two children's books. His main works include *No Free Sleeping*, *In the Name of Amandla, Magicstan Fires, Handsome Jita, Bilakhulu! Longer Poems*. He won 2nd place of Sol Plaatje European Union Poetry Prize in 2012 and 2013.

曼德拉，你有没有想过？

你有没有想过
当我们收拾死尸，沉重的
丑陋残酷的过去的重担
威胁着要窒息我们，
开始马萨卡纳运动
重新人性化地球上体弱多病的街头儿童
将迷失的灵魂置于关爱的金色阳光下，
地球村因金钱疯狂而流血？

你有没有想过
当我们修补百年历史的
新鲜的、巨人的伤口，
关闭曾经像埃博拉病毒一样侵蚀生命的
布满弹孔的
建筑物
那么多人在舒适的花园里放松——
在电红色羽绒被里做爱？

Mandela, Have You Ever Wondered?

Have you ever wondered
As we pick up the dead, heavy
Weight of the ugly brutal past
That threatens to suffocate us,
Embarking on the Masakhane campaign
Rehumanising sickly-frail street children of the earth
Placing detoured souls under the caring golden sun,
That the global village bleeds from money madness?

Have you ever wondered
As we patch centuries-old
Fresh, gaping wounds,
Closing pockmarked cannonhole-riddled
Buildings that once eroded life like ebola
That so many relax in cosy gardens –
In electrific red duvets and make love?

你有没有想过

当你抓挠皮肤时

寻找你的独特之处——你自己

胜利的人群退居贫民窟？

你有没有想过？

（范静哗 译）

Have you ever wondered

As you scratch your skin

Searching for your uniqueness – your own self

That the triumphant crowd retires to ghettos?

Have you ever wondered?

walking
行　走

姆多利西·涅祖瓦　科萨语、英语诗人，南非多语种期刊《库塔兹》编辑。已出版诗集《歌曲选拔赛》《新国家》等，以及回忆录《布拉瓦无法抚慰的灵魂》。曾获 1999 年伊丽莎白-哥德堡港诗歌奖、2001 年托马斯·普林格尔诗歌奖、2008 年戏剧艺术文学权保组织诗歌奖、2009 年南非文学奖等奖项。

Mxolisi Nyezwa
姆多利西·涅祖瓦

Mxolisi Nyezwa (b.1967) is an Xhosa poet and editor of *Kotaz*, a multilingual South African journal. He has published poetry collections *Song Trials* (2000), *New Country* (2008), *Malikhanye* (2011), *Poems from the Earth* (2017), *Ndiyoyika* (2018) and memoir *Bhlawa's Inconsolable Spirits* (2023). He is the laureate of Port Elizabeth-Gothenburg Poetry Prize (1999), Thomas Pringle Poetry Award (2001), Dalro Poetry Prize (2008), and South African Literary Award (2009).

行 走

我一动不动。我在我的衬衫和元素中,
感受到静脉颤动, 心脏跳动,
杂草穿过头骨, 穿过头骨周围的
一片空气。

我看到黑暗海洋的不可靠, 愤怒,
在我脊背、脊柱、脊椎的天空。
我盯着陌生人冷漠的眼睛看,
盯着那隐约的幽默, 地球被遗忘的微笑。

我走在一条不拐弯的街道。
我击落一只鸟的翅膀。我看到一个宇宙
从破损的天空俯冲下来。我脚步不停。
我看到人们向着毫不移动的人群盘旋。

(范静哗 译)

walking

i keep still. in my shirt and in my element
i feel the vein's tremor, the heart's pulse,
the weed through the skull, through a piece of air
around my skull.

i see the unstable dark sea, furious
and on my back, my spine, the vertebral sky.
i look the cold stranger in the eye,
the looming humor, earth's forgotten smiles.

i walk the length in an unbending street.
i knock down a bird's wing. i see a universe
speeding down a broken sky. i don't stop.
i see men circling towards an unmoving crowd.

جوان
Молодость
青春 Youth
जवानी الشباب
Juventude

沙特阿拉伯

Saudi Arabia

حارسة السر
秘密的守护者

苏尔坦·戴特 诗人、作家。拉卡什出版和发行公司创始人兼总经理，阿拉伯历史学者。作品有口语诗《墨云2020》，古典诗词《罗盘无北》，小说《众神草地——猛犸象》。参与涉及历史题材电影剧本创作。曾获2021年阿拉伯世界"诗人王子"诗歌比赛第一名。

Sultan Saud Alotaibi

苏尔坦·戴特

Sultan Saud Alotaibi (b.1993) serves in Raqash Publishing and Distribution, Saudi Ministry of Culture. He is a poet and creative writer who has published three poetry collections and one play. As a scholar on Arabic history, he is the founder and director of Dar Raqash Publishing and Distribution. He won first place in the largest Arab poetry competition "Prince of Poets" in 2021.

秘密的守护者

因为你是她的最后一个幸存者
你将在六个方向，被从她处流放

她将强行在你身上进出
把你丧子的灵魂支配于指掌

她在黑夜劈开你肢体的幻想
再显现出一个你不曾造就的太阳

你最好没有在心底对她不忠
因为生与死都不能将你包藏

你对她示以皮壳就默默离去
当她召唤你时你竟不予帮忙

当她来临，她是来贯穿一切：
你的皮壳、想法，以及最深的真相

حارسة السر

لأنكَ آخرُ الناجينَ.. منها
ستُنفى في الجهات الست عنها

ستخرجُ منكَ.. تدخلُ فيكَ قسراً
وتأمرُ روحَك الثكلى وتنهى

تشقُ خيالَك الجسديَّ ليلاً
وتظهرُ منهُ شمساً لم تُبنها

فلا موتٌ يقيكَ ولا حياةٌ
فليتَكَ في ضميرك لم تخنها

تباديها قشوراً ثمَّ تمضي
وإذ أعطتَكَ وصلاً لم تعنها

وحين أتتكَ جاءتكَ اختراقاً
قشوراً ثمَّ عمقاً ثمَّ كُنها

她总是给你罩上一圈光晕
可你却从她身上驱散光亮

只要可能，她就周济你的困难
当她需要你的援手，你却吝惜钱粮

在那里，在那永恒中，她曾
为你构成一瞬，你却无视和珍藏

放轻脚步吧，但要敬畏她的步伐
切不要将她蔑视，自我膨胀

你终将随风而去，那就做一股空气
山岚将为你披上衣裳，那就做一片山岗

（韩誉 译，薛庆国 校译）

تحيطُكَ هالةً بالضوء دوماً
وأنتَ تُبدِّدُ الأضواءَ عنها

تُدينك دائماً منذُ استطاعت
وكانت في يديكَ ولم تُدنها

هناكَ.. هناكَ.. في الأبدي
كانت تُشكِّلُ لحظةً لكَ لم تحنها

تخفف من خُطاك وخف خُطاها
ولا تُكبِر أناكَ ولا تُهنها

ستحملُكَ الرياحُ فكن هواءً
وتلبسك الجبالُ غداً فكنها

محاولات عديدة لقول الشيء نفسه
说出同一件事的多次尝试

拉万·塔拉勒　诗人、专栏作家、文化项目经理。曾任利雅得公共卫生局医学实验室专家。她出版有诗集《微笑的屋顶女孩》等。诗歌选入《30 位诗人，30 首诗——沙特青年诗歌选》和法译沙特诗选《在风沙的奔腾中》。曾参加突尼斯国际诗歌节、沙特吉达书展"101 个词语：巴拉德诗歌之夜"等活动。

青春，如风有信

Rawan Talal
拉万·塔拉勒

Rawan Talal (b.1992) is a poet, columnist and cultural project manager, once served as a medical laboratory specialist of Public Health Authority of Riyadh. She has published poetry selection *The Roof Girl Smiling*, and her works are included in anthologies *30 Poets, 30 Poems* and *Dans les galops du sable*. She attended Jeddah Book Fair, Sidi Bou Said International Poetry Festival of Tunisia and "101 Words: Poetry Night in Al-Balad".

说出同一件事的多次尝试

同一个词语的无限重复
经过时间的训练，能让词语每一次
都产生新的声音

大量的练习
能让黑夜走出洞窟
时而向着光
时而向着孤独的人
反复创造他的败绩……

走向海洋的黑夜
记得溺水者们的姓名
慷慨地守护着
他们漂浮的梦想……

走向河流的黑夜
将弗吉尼亚·伍尔夫带回岸边

محاولات عديدة لقول الشيء نفسه

تكرار دائم لكلمة واحدة
يمرنها الوقت لتخرج في كل مرة
بوقع جديد

تمرين مكثف
ليخرج الليل من كهفه
مرة باتجاه الضوء
ومرة باتجاه الوحيد
يعيد خلق هزائمه..

ليل باتجاه البحر
يحفظ أسماء الغرقى
ويحرس برحابة
أحلامهم الطافية..

ليل باتجاه النهر
يعيد فرجينيا وولف لليابسة

抛去所有

苦难的石头……

大量的练习

能让黑夜走出洞窟

成为比存在更早一步的

第一黑夜

保持着寻找它自己意义的先机。

（韩誉 译，薛庆国 校译）

متخلصا من كل الحجارة

المعذبة..

تمرين مكثف

ليخرج الليل من كهفه

الليل الأول

سابقا الوجود بخطوة

ومحتفظا بسبق البحث عما يعنيه.

احرقوني
焚烧我

哈特姆·谢赫里　诗人、出版代理、电视主持人。有 16 年出版业工作经验，担任 2022 年利雅得国际书展奖评委会成员，诺拉公主大学英语文学系项目咨询委员会成员。著有 16 本书，作品被翻译成英语、法语、西班牙语、瑞典语、意大利语等。曾获 2019 年沙特阿拉伯短篇小说奖。

Hatim Alshehri

哈特姆·谢赫里

Hatim Alshehri (b.1989) is a poet, literary agent and TV host. He has published 16 books. With working experience of 16 years in publishing business, he was the judge of the Riyadh International Book Fair Prize and a member of Project Consultation Committee, Princess Nora bint Abdul Rahman University. He won the second place in Short Story Award of Saudi Arabia 2019. His works have been translated into English, French, Spanish, Swedish, Italian, etc.

焚烧我

在我周围堆起柴火，焚烧我！

我是叛教者的后裔，我的爷爷是个江湖巫医

只不过他不是独眼 *

重要的是，焚烧我！

死在火中就是胜出，然后请埋葬我！

我有脖子，我有罪行

要怎样才能走上断头台？

如果你们缺少木柴，给你们

我的部落，他们就是你们可以点燃的柴火

我是罪人，理应葬身烈火

人们啊，快来点燃柴火！

在你们点火之前，我早已死去

你们的火杀死的是你们自己

当你们收拾、掩埋我的碎骨

绿草将长满我的坟墓；大地会说：

天呐，你们怎么埋葬了诗歌……

（韩誉 译，薛庆国 校译）

* 译注：伊斯兰教圣训中末日前出现的伪救世主称作"麦西哈 · 旦扎里"，麦西哈意为基督、救世主，旦扎里意为在江湖上行骗者，"麦西哈 · 旦扎里"的形象是一个独眼龙。

احرقوني

أجمعوا الأعواد حولي واحرقوني..

أنا من سلالة مارق/ دجال جدي

لكنه ليس بأعور..

المهم أحرقوني..

فاز الذي بالنار مات، رجاء ادفنوني..

كيف السبيل إلى المقصلة/

عنقي وأخطائي معي..

إن كان ينقصكم حطب/ هذي

قبيلتي، جند من الحطب أشعلوها..

أنا مذنب والنار حقي، هيا يا رجال

أشعلوها..

أنا ميّت من قبل إشعال النار،

ناركم تميتكم أنتم..

حينما تجمعون رفاتي وتدفنوني

سيعشوشب القبر؛ وتقول الأرض:

الله كيف دفنتم القصيدة..

نهاية أسبوع في الجنة
天堂的周末

胡达·穆巴拉克　诗人、编剧。沙特费萨尔国王专科医院和研究中心高级理疗师。已出版两本阿拉伯语诗集。在多个本地和国际文学期刊上发表诗歌。参加过 2015 年瑞典古腾堡诗歌节等多场国内外诗歌活动。参与联合编剧、电视节目前期制作工作，2022 年担任短片《豪德》的剧本总监。

青春，如风有信

Huda Almubarak

胡达·穆巴拉克

Huda Almubarak (b.1988) is a poet and scriptwriter, serving as senior physiotherapist of King Faisal Specialist Hospital and Research Center. She is the author of two poetry books in Arabic, main writer of short film and co-writer of TV show pre-productions. She attended a lot of poetry events at home and abroad during the last decade, including Gutenberg Poetry Festival-Sweden 2015. Her poems were published in many local and international literature journals.

天堂的周末

我重新准备，

初次的被造，

那时，一切皆有可能，

比预计的更容易，

细到无法看见，

广到无法命名，

轻到无法听出，

在过客的视线中，

我以它作赌。

愿河流怜悯干渴，

愿生命善待天堂的一个周末，

尽管我有可能成为一座花园，

可你选择了山，

快过撞碎在月球上的光，

暖过稍感无聊的太阳，

强过海洋里的一粒盐，

美过调戏命运的少女，

نهاية أسبوع في الجنة

أعيد التهيئة..

للصنعة الأولى،

حيث كان كل شيء ممكنا،

أبسط مما أتوقع،

أرقُ من أن يُرى،

أشملَ من أن يسمّى،

وأخفت من أن يُسمع،

راهنتُ به،

بين نظرات العابرين..

علّ الأنهار تشفق على العطشى،

علّ الحياة تتعطف بـ نهاية أسبوع في الجنة،

مع إمكانية أن أكون حديقة،

لكنك أخترت الجبل،

أسرع من ضوء ينكسر على القمر،

أكثر دفئا من شمس تشعر بالملل،

أقوى من ذرة ملح في البحر،

أجمل من طفلة تشاغب القدر،

最有趣的故事将在 2020 年被讲述

比怜爱的眼光更柔，

他抵抗……他假装无视……他抵抗……

他伸出双臂问好

他责备自己，深呼吸!

我不是孤身一人

无论如何我都将燃烧

就让我的燃烧成为艺术吧。

（韩誉 译，薛庆国 校译）

أظرف قصة ستُقال عن عام ٢٠٢٠
أحنُّ من نظرة حب،
قاوم.. تجاهل.. قاوم..
مدّ ذراعيه مسلّما..
شتم نفسه، نفسٌ عميق!
لم أكن وحدي..
سأحترق بجميع الأحوال،
فليكن احتراقيّ فنّا.

جوان
Молодость
青春 Youth
جوانी الشباب
Juventude

Egypt 埃及

سبعُ وظائف لا تُلائِمُني
七种不适合我的职业

穆罕默德·穆塔亚姆　诗人、记者、文学编辑、纪录片电影制作人，巴勒斯坦文化平台艾尔伊斯提克拉尔新闻总编辑。曾攻读药学专业，后在开罗戏剧艺术高等研究院学习戏剧与评论。作品有《开门吧，法蒂玛》《一滴眼泪打破两次围攻》。曾获"穆罕默德·阿菲菲·马塔尔"古典诗歌奖第一名，以及 2019 年 2 月在开罗举行的阿拉伯青年创意节上获阿拉伯世界古典诗歌第一名。

Mohamed Elmotayam
穆罕默德·穆塔亚姆

Mohamed Elmotayam (b.1993) is a freelance journalist, literary editor, documentary filmmaker and contributor to Al-Istiqlal Cultural Platform. He studied pharmacy, then drama and criticism at the Higher Institute of Theatrical Arts in Cairo. He is the author of two published collections, *Open the Door, Fatima* and *A Tear Breaks Two Sieges*. He got the first in the "Muhammad Afifi Matar" Prize for Classical Poetry and first place in Arab world in classical poetry at the Arab Youth Creativity Festival held in Cairo in February 2019.

七种不适合我的职业

他说: 做个雕塑家吧

我说: 去滋扰石头的宁静吗?

他说: 那就做一只鸟

我说: 去叫醒游子的思念吗?

他说: 那就做个乐手

我说: 去揭露木头的忧伤, 而不是掩盖它吗?

他说: 那就做一条街道

我说: 去承受负债者的踩踏吗?

他说: 那就做一个山丘

我说: 我怜悯跛脚的痴情人

他说: 那就做黑夜

我说: 长了也要被骂, 短了也要被骂

而我既不能变长, 又不能变短

他说: 那就做……

我说: 让我……做个守墓人吧

去带着谦卑聆听虚无

背靠墓碑

伸直双腿

永恒

枕着我的大腿, 昏昏欲睡。

（韩誉 译，薛庆国 校译）

سبعُ وظائف لا تُلائِمُني

قال: كُنْ نحّاتًا..

قلتُ: وأزعجُ سكونَ الحَجَر؟!

قال: فكُنْ طيرًا..

قلتُ: وأوقظُ حنينَ المهاجر؟!

قال: فكُنْ عازفًا..

قلتُ: وأُفشي حزنَ الخشبةِ بدلًا مِنْ ضَمِّها؟!

قال: فكُنْ شارعًا..

قلتُ: أوَأحتَمِل ثقَلَ خطوةِ المَدين؟!

قال: فكُنْ ربوَةً..

قلتُ: أُشفِقُ على العاشق الأعرج!

قال: فكُنْ الليل..

قلتُ: إن طُلتُ لَعنوني وإن قصُرتُ لَعنوني،

وما بيَ طولٌ ولا قِصَر..!

قال: كُنْ....

قلتُ: اجعلني... حارسَ جبّانةٍ،

أُصغي بخشوعٍ للعدم،

ظهري مسنودٌ إلى شاهدِ قبر،

ساقاي ممدودتان،

والأبديةُ..

تضَعُ رأسَها على فَخذي وتَنْعَس.

كل شيء في مكانه الصحيح
一切都在它正确的地方

阿拉·哈桑·福达 诗人。毕业于亚历山大大学药学院。著有诗集
《狼嚎的嘶哑》《子宫顶部的痣》等。曾获埃及文学新闻奖。曾
参加巴黎阿拉伯世界研究所举行的诗歌朗诵会等国内国际活动。
诗歌散见于埃及和其它阿拉伯国家期刊。

Alaa Hassan Fouda

阿拉·哈桑·福达

Alaa Hassan Fouda (b.1991), a poet and pharmacist who graduated from Alexandria University. She is the author of two poetry collections, *The Hoarseness of Wolf's Howl* and *A Mole at the Top of Uterus*. She has won the Literature News Prize of Egypt, and she participated in poetry reading at the Arab World Institute in Paris. Her works were published in journals in Egypt and other Arabic countries.

一切都在它正确的地方

灰尘在地毯下堆积

炮弹被墙纸覆盖

盘子上的腐败, 盖着白色的毛巾

袜子上的补丁被鞋隐藏

鞋底的破洞被路遮挡

悲惨在家庭合影背后

爱在相机的闪光灯前

一切都在它正确的地方

优秀毕业生的证书在失业者的房间里

婚礼的主角因为到了结婚年龄而做爱

家庭主妇不相信现成的酱汁

所以她亲手在屋顶下发明了它

乳牙干净的孩子喝牛奶

MBC2 电视台* 删除不当画面

我们很可能会在六十岁时死去

我们中的一个人将在社保大楼附近向另一个人挥手

你会对我说: 我们在体验生活

---

* 译注: 沙特的国有电影频道。

كل شيء في مكانه الصحيح

التراب مُكومٌ تحت السجادة
القذائف مغطاةٌ بورق الحائط
العفن في الأطباق تعلوه مناشفَ بيضاء
الرتق في الجورب يخفيه الحذاء
والثقب في الحذاء يستره الطريق
التعاسة وراء الصورة العائلية
والحب أمام فلاش الكاميرا
كل شيء في مكانه الصحيح
شهادةٌ جامعية بمرتبة الشرف في غرفة عاطلٍ عن العمل
حفلُ زفافٍ بطلاه يمارسان الحب لأنهما بلغا سن الزواج
ربةُ منزلٍ لا تثق في الصلصة الجاهزة
فتخترعها أمام عينيها تحت سقف البيت
أطفالٌ بأسنان لبنيةٍ نظيفةٍ يشربون الحليب
وقناة MBC2 تحذف المشاهد غير اللائقة
سنموت في الستين على الأرجح
أحدنا سيلوح للآخر على مقربة من مبنى التأمينات الاجتماعية
ستقول لي: كنا نجرب الحياة

我会告诉你：这个产品是一次性的

你会向我谈起那些已经长大成人的孩子们

我会给你讲讲电影《革命之路》

你把骨头的颤抖藏在外套下

我向世界释放我的皱纹

一切都在它正确的地方

花瓶里的玫瑰

笼子里的鸟

书架上的书

桌子上的餐巾

够二十个人用的勺子

而时间，这个混蛋，不等游戏结束就关了灯

你对我说：一切都在它正确的地方

我对你说：一切都在它正确的地方。

（韩誉 译，薛庆国 校译）

سأقول لك: هذا المنتج صالحٌ للاستخدام مرةً واحدة

ستحدثني عن الأطفال الذين صاروا شباباً

سأحدثك عن فيلم revolutionary road

أنت تُخبئ ارتعاشة عظامك خلف المعطف

وأنا أطلق تجاعيدي للعالم

كل شيء في مكانه الصحيح

الوردة في الڤازة

العصفور في القفص

الكتب على الأرفف

المناديل فوق الطاولات

والملاعق تكفي عشرين شخصًا

والزمن هذا الوغد أطفأ الأنوار قبل أن تنتهي اللعبة

تقول لي: كل شيء في مكانه الصحيح

أقول لك: كل شيء في مكانه الصحيح.

رغبات

渴望

哈桑·阿米尔　诗人。毕业于基纳南谷大学文学院英语系。出版有诗集五种，包括《我用黑血写作》《牧羊人的午睡》等。他曾获得埃及文化部国家鼓励奖、卡塔拉奖，阿拉伯世界"诗人王子"诗歌比赛第三名。

Hassan Amer

哈桑·阿米尔

Hassan Amer (b.1989), poet, graduated from the Department of English literature, South Valley University. He is the author of five poetry selections including *I Write in Black Blood*, and *Flockmaster's Afternoon Nap*. He has won the State Encouragement Award for Poetry from Egyptian Ministry of Culture, Katara Award and the third place in the "Prince of Poets" Competition in 2017.

渴望

我有一种渴望

渴望失去一切

渴望遗忘和被遗忘

渴望端详世界的原样

从一个未知的小镇开始

渴望有个女人不知道我的思念

或是在去往推迟的车站的

车厢门口, 将我送别

渴望伙伴们平分了我的记忆

再将我忘记

渴望在万物眼中永远轻稀

我有一种渴望, 渴望向过客谢绝一切

或是离去, 并将地方留给他人

对沙漠, 我有一种难以名状的思念

那里, 土地宽广

心朝所有方向敞开

在词语开始之前

除了这辽阔的宁静, 我别无所求。

（韩誉 译，薛庆国 校译）

رغبات

بي رغبةٌ
أن أفقدَ الأشياءَ،
أنْ أَنْسَى وأنْ أُنْسَى،
وأن أتأمَّلَ الدنيا كما هيَ/
شارعًا في بلدة مجهولةٍ.
أن تُنْكِرَ امرأةٌ حنيني،
أو تودِّعَني على باب القطارِ
إلى محطاتٍ مُؤَجَّلَة،
وأنْ يتقاسمَ الأصحابُ ذاكرتي وينسوَني،
وأنْ أبقى خفيفًا في عيونِ الكائناتْ
بي رغبةٌ في الاعتذارِ لعابرٍ عن أيِّ شيءٍ،
أو مغادرة المكانِ لآخرينَ
وبي حنينٌ غامضُ الأسبابِ للصحراء
حيثُ الأرضُ واسعةٌ
وحيث القلبُ مفتوحُ الجهاتْ
لا شيءَ ينقصُني سوى هذا السكونِ الرَّحبِ
قبلَ بدايةِ الكلماتْ.

أبحث عن كلمات لم يكتبها الشعراء
"我寻找诗人未曾写过的词语"

艾哈迈德·扎卡里亚　诗人、译者，2009 年本科毕业于开罗大学阿拉伯文学专业。曾担任《新阿拉伯人报》驻土耳其新闻记者，发表过诸多有关土耳其和阿拉伯文化的文章和译作。已出版诗集《辩证法》《那些不能对说另一种语言的人说的话》。曾获 2015 年马哈茂德·达尔维什博物馆诗歌奖、2020—2021 年度伊本·白图泰旅行文学奖。现居安卡拉。

青春，如风有信

Ahmet Zekeriya
艾哈迈德·扎卡里亚

Ahmet Zekeriya (b.1984) is a poet and translator with a Bachelor's degree in Arabic literature from the University of Cairo in 2009. Served once as a journalist of *Al-Arabi Al-Jadeed*, he has published many articles on Arabic and Turkish cultures as well as poetry collections *Jidaliyya* and *What I Couldn't Say to Anyone in Another Language*. Besides, he has translated several Turkish literary works into Arabic. He is the laureate of Ibn Battuta Prize for Travel Literature (2020-2021) and Mahmoud Darwish Museum Poetry Prize in 2015. Now he lives in Ankara.

"我寻找诗人未曾写过的词语"

我寻找诗人未曾写过的词语

在远离诗人国度的地方……

我寻找不试图从课本中

删去春天的国度……

我寻找未被士兵从歌手喉中夺取的

新的歌曲

我寻找下套猎捕思念的诗

哪怕思念的是我的母亲

——我唯一热爱的笃信一教派的人，她只为我和全体

　穆斯林祷告

我寻找母语的另一种意义

寻找另一根舌头，它不会

用一种语言思考，再用另一种语言表达……

我寻找新的记忆，它不会

寻找一个从不问我境况的国家。

（韩誉 译，薛庆国 校译）

أبحث عن كلماتٍ لم يكتبها الشعراء

أبحث عن كلماتٍ لم يكتبها الشعراء

بعيداً عن بلادهم..

أبحث عن بلادٍ لا تحاول أن تحذف الربيعَ

من الكتب المدرسية..

أبحث عن أغنية جديدة

لم يقتلعها العساكرُ من حناجر المُغَنِّين..

أبحث عن قصيدة تنصب الفخاخَ للحنين،

حتى إلى أمي

الطائفية الوحيدة التي أحببتُها، وهي تدعو اللهَ لي

وللمسلمين فقط..

أبحث عن معنى آخر لِلغتي الأَمِّ..

وعن لسانٍ آخر

لا يفكر بلغة، ويتحدث بأخرى..

أبحث عن ذاكرةٍ جديدةٍ

لا تبحث عن بلاد لا تسأل عني.

في سن السادسة والستين
在六十六岁

娜贾特·阿里 诗人、散文家、文学评论家，现任埃及最高文化委员会出版部主任。著有诗集《爱唠叨的迷信生物》《有裂缝的墙》《犹如刀刃》《玻璃坟墓》《时间：孤独之外》，以及评论集《纳吉布·马哈富兹小说中的叙述者》《尤素福·伊德里斯短篇小说中的反讽》。散文和评论散见于各报纸刊物。曾获埃及文化部最佳诗集奖、"贝鲁特 39"奖、摩洛哥丹吉尔诗歌奖等。作品被翻译成英、法、西、瑞、葡等多种语言。曾多次参加在法国、瑞典、比利时、委内瑞拉、美国举办的诗歌节和文学工作坊。

Nagat Ali
娜贾特·阿里

Nagat Ali (b.1973) is a poet, essayist and literary critic, working as the general supervisor of publishing, Supreme Council of Culture. Her works include poetry selections *A Superstitious Creature Adores Garrulousness*, *Cracked Wall*, *Like the Blade of Knife*, *Glass Tomb*, *Time Is Out of Solitude* and criticism collections *The Narrator in the Novels of Naguib Mahfouz* and *The Irony in the Short Stories of Yusuf Idris*. Her essays and reviews are published in many newspapers and magazines. She is the laureate of Egyptian Ministry of Culture Prize for Poetry, Beirut 39 Prize, Tangier Prize for Poetry in Morocco, etc. Her works have been translated into English, French, Spanish, Swedish, Portuguese and so on. She attended many poetry festivals and workshops in France, Sweden, Belgium, Venezuela and the US.

在六十六岁

在六十六岁
你将玩弄你还剩下的
年月
你将把你未来的日子
称为"荒废时间"
看人们从海上失败归来
将成为你的消遣
你将嘲弄爱情
是它蹉跎了你的岁月
让你在睡梦中间
恐惧地苏醒
但这些都绝不会耽误你
在临屋发出呓语的
尸体中间
散步游玩
以便抵抗孤独的幽灵
你将永远

في سن السادسة والستين

في سن السادسة والستين
ستلهو بما تبقى لديك
من الزمن
وستسمي أيامكَ القادمة
بـ «الوقت الضائع»
وستتسلى بالفرجة على
خسارة العائدين من البحر
وتسخر من الحب
الذي ضيعكَ سنينًا
فجعلك تستيقظُ خائفًا
في منتصف الحلم
لكن هذا لن يمنعَك أبدًا
من التنزه بين بقايا
الجثث التي تهذي
في الغرف المجاورة
كي تقاوم أشباح الوحدة
وستفخر دوما بأنك

为自己创造了足够的传奇

而感到自豪

在六十六岁

你将为城市的状况痛苦

——在你不经意间，它已经衰老

你将取笑女孩

为你点燃蜡烛的模样

以此来驱散瞌睡

天长日久

只有这瞌睡仍坚信你

尚未死去。

（韩誉 译，薛庆国 校译）

قد صنعتَ ما يكفيك

من الأساطير

في سن السادسة والستين

ستؤلمك أيضا حال المدينة

التي شاختْ دون أن تنتبه لها

و ستتندر على مشهد البنت

التي أوقدتْ لك شمعة

كي تبدد تلك الغفلة

التي طالتْ

وظلتْ تؤمن بأنك

لم تمتْ بعدُ.

أحدثُ عروض السيرك
最新的马戏表演

谢里夫·沙菲伊　诗人，《金字塔报》记者。出版有诗集《在他们两人之间，时间变得生锈》《他独自一人聆听化学音乐会》《色彩震撼》《机器人的完整收藏》《仿佛月亮围绕着我》等和法语译作集《值得一读的风》《烟雾带来的消息》。另有诗歌被翻译成英语、意大利语等。他曾获得埃及文艺总局奖，参加过法国、美国、摩洛哥、约旦、黎巴嫩、沙特、科威特等国的诗歌活动。

Sharif Al-Shafiey
谢里夫·沙菲伊

Sharif Al-Shafiey (b.1972) is a poet and journalist working in Al-Ahram Newspaper, Cairo. He is the author *of Between the Two of Them*, *Time Gets Rusty* (1994), *All by Himself*, *He Listens to the Concert of Chemistry* (1996), *Colors Tremble Covetously* (1999), *The Complete Collection of a Robot* (2008-2012) and *As if a Moon Surrounding Me* (2013), and two French translation books *Un Vent digne d'être lu* (2014), *Messages portés par la fumée* (2016). Some of his poems are also translated into English and Italian. He is the laureate of the Award of The General Authority of Cultural Palaces, and he attended many poetry festivals in France, the US, Morocco, Jordan, Lebanon, Saudi Arabia and Kuwait.

最新的马戏表演

我一般不为马戏表演感到享受
因为那些动物让我想起我
不情愿而兽化的自己
高难动作吸引不了我这样的
每天走钢丝的
与月亮、毒蛇、烟雾共舞的杂技演员

最近一次演出中让我真正惊奇的、
被我爱人说成"可怕"的
是群狮造反的场面
它们突然袭击了驯兽师
没有飞扑，没有撕咬
而是用鞭打
命令他优雅地穿过火圈
因为他才是驯化的大史诗中
值得活着、接受喝彩的新的主演

（韩誉 译，薛庆国 校译）

أحدثُ عروضِ السيرك

لا أستمتعُ عادةً بعروضِ السّيركِ
فالوحوشُ تُذكّرُني بذاتي،
التي توحَّشَتْ رغْمًا عني
والحركاتُ الصعبةُ لا تجتذبُ بهلوانًا مثلي
يمشي على الحبالِ يوميًا
ويراقصُ القمرَ والأفاعي والدخانَ

الذي أَدْهَشَني حقًّا في العرضِ الأخيرِ
وَوَصَفَتْهُ حبيبتي بأنه «مُرْعِبٌ»
هو مشْهدُ الأسُودِ المتمرّدة
التي هَجَمَتْ فجْأةً على مدرّبها
وبدلاً من أن تَنْهَشَهُ أو تحاولَ افتراسَهُ
ضَرَبَتْهُ بالكرباج
وَطَلَبَتْ منه أن يمرَّ برشاقةٍ من «طَوْقِ النّار»
باعتباره البطلَ الجديدَ لملحمةِ الترويضِ الْكُبْرَى،
الذي يَسْتَحِقُّ الحياةَ وتحيّةَ الْجُمهورِ

البيت
房子

艾哈迈德·叶麦尼　诗人、翻译家。西班牙、埃及双重国籍。曾任西班牙马德里康普顿斯大学副教授，现在在西班牙国际广播电台工作。已出版六本阿拉伯语诗集，一本西班牙语诗集。1991年，他被埃及文化部和法国开罗中心授予"兰波"奖，于2010年获"贝鲁特39"奖。诗歌被翻译成英、法、德、西、波、意等多种语言。参加过世界各地多个诗歌节和朗诵会，并将西班牙和拉丁美洲著名当代诗人的诗集翻译成阿拉伯语。

Ahmed Yamani
艾哈迈德·叶麦尼

Ahmed Yamani (b.1970) is currently a programmer and anchor in the International Spanish Radio, served once as an associate professor of Universidad Complutense de Madrid. He has published six poetry books in Arabic and has published a poetry collection translated into Spanish. He is the winner of Arthur Rimbaud Prize in 1991 from the Ministry of Culture in Egypt and the French Institute in Cairo, Beirut 39 Award in 2010. His works have been translated into English, French, German, Spanish, Polish, Italian, Romanian and Ukrainian. He has participated in many poetry festivals and poetry readings in a lot of countries. He has translated a number of works by famous poets of Spain and Latin America into Arabic.

房子

他用沙子盖房，然后用脚踩踏。

用纸板盖房，然后用手撕碎。

用木头盖房，一截取暖的蜡烛将它烧光。

用铁皮盖房，请了同街区的一个朋友帮忙，

他们为产权争执不清，于是两家将房子无情摧毁。

在市区边缘，他用石头另盖了一栋房子

被一群山里的荷枪实弹者占领

他们拆了房子，用来修高速公路

深夜，他返回出生的地方

没找到房子，只认出几只鸽子

等着他来投喂几颗麦粒，或是一点水。

（韩誉 译，薛庆国 校译）

البيت

صنع بيتاً من الرمل ثم داسه بقدميه.

من الكرتون، ومزّقه بيديه.

من الخشب، شمعة كان يتدفأ بها أحرقته.

من الصفيح، بمساعدة أحد أصدقاء الحيّ،

اختلفا على ملكيّته، فحطمته العائلتان دون هوادة.

صنع آخرَ من الحجر على طرف المدينة

احتلّه حاملو الأسلحة.

من الجبل، دكّوه لإقامة أوتوستراد.

عاد ليلاً إلى حيث سقطت رأسه

ولم يجد البيت، فقط تعرف على بضع حمامات

كانت تتطلع إليه ليلقي إليها حبة قمح أو شربة ماء.

جوان

Молодость

青 春 Youth

जवानी الشباب

Juventude

United Arab Emirates 阿联酋

عن حُريّة السُقوط
关于坠落的自由

法蒂玛·巴德尔　诗人，保险公司创新官。9岁开始写作，已出版诗集《黎明自尽之前》《铁锈的味道》。

Fatima Badr
法蒂玛·巴德尔

Fatima Badr (b.1997), poet, working as the Innovation Officer of Alliance Insurance Company. She began her writing journey at nine years old. She has published two poetry selections, *Before Dawn Hangs Itself* (2020) and *The Taste of Rust* (2022).

关于坠落的自由

第一次
我试图捕获走失的呼吸
头痛,从它的死者身边拿走悲伤的伞
我被我的骨头落在身后,陷入脆弱
我的皮在紧缩的寺院张灯结彩
在我体内研磨永恒的构成。

这假设
这古老的饥饿
那被阉割的距离
一座远离我拥抱的桥
一副身躯
以边际为食粮
居高临下
仿佛想要跃起
赤身裸体地
去它幻象的坟墓

عن حُريّة السُقوط

للمَرة الأُولى
أُحاولُ اصطيادَ أنفاسي التائهة
صُداعي الذي يَحملُ مَظلَّة الأسى عن مَوتَاه
تَأخرتُ عن عظامي حتى ارتَطَمْتُ بالهَشاشة
جلدي الذي يُقيم احتفالاتهُ في دير التقلُّص
ويَطحنُ فيَّ التكوّنَ الأبديّ.

—

هذا الافتراضْ
هذا الجُوع القَديم
تلكَ المَسافةُ الخصيّة
جسْرٌ بَعيدٌ عن عِناقي
جَسدٌ وحيدٌ
يَقتاتُ على الحَافة
يطلُّ من الأعلى
كَمْا لو أنّهُ يَنوي الوُثوبَ
إلى قبره الوَهميّ
مُتجردًا من رداءته

我的神啊

从我的白色

我的透明中

啜饮你的尘埃

好让我的存在, 渗漏为

语言的

收益

在空的运行中

在坠落的自由中

无怨无悔。

（韩誉 译, 薛庆国 校译）

—

إلهــي
اشرَبْ من بَياضي..
شَفافِيَتي
غُبارَكَ
كيْ يَتَسَرَّب وُجودي،
في جَدوَى
اللّغة
في حَرَكَة الفَراغ
في حُريّة السُقوطِ
بِلا نَدمْ.

ترهُّل..

涣 散

哈桑·纳贾尔 诗人，沙迦大学阿拉伯语言文学博士，现任阿联酋人力资源和酋长国文化部官员。著有诗集《我们脱去门阶上的影子》《枕边一抹忧愁》《灵魂的鸽子》《镜子的乡愁》。曾获 2020 年突尼斯阿拉伯学生诗人论坛金羽毛奖。曾参加 2009 年"诗人王子"诗歌比赛及多个阿联酋国内外诗歌节活动。

Hassan Alnajjar

哈桑·纳贾尔

Hassan Alnajjar (b.1984), poet, is currently the First Labor Inspector of Mohre. He is the author of four poetry collections, *We Talk Off Shadow on the Doorstep*, *On His Pillow Is A Touch of Anxiety*, *Soul's Pigeons* and *Nostalgia of Mirrors*. He is the laureate of Golden Feather Prize on the Arab Student Poets Forum in Tunisia in 2020. He attended many poetry festivals and cultural events at home and abroad, including "Prince of Poets" Competition 2009.

涣 散

岁月涣散了他的精神
像缆绳在水上变松、变长
在无名小舟上飘飘荡荡。

他在无数双手之间摇摆不定
将命运交给了线，任它们操弄
这里一下，那里一下
却不知接下来去往何方？！

别人的愿望将他到处拉扯
周遭唯独他寸草不生
却没有人将雨水分享。

一旦希望萌出枝叶
早有镰刀守候一旁
他的灵魂是一个剧场
关了灯，息了声
撞门声久久回荡
黑夜在寂静中延伸、拉长。

（韩誉 译，薛庆国 校译）

ترهُّل..

روحُهُ تَتَرَهَّلُ من أثر الوقت
مثلَ حِبالٍ تراختْ على صفحةِ الماءِ
يلهو بها قاربٌ مهمَلٌ.

يتأرجحُ بين الأيادي
ويُسلِّمُ أقدارَهُ للخيوطِ التي تتلاعبُ فيهِ
فتحملُهُ جهةٌ تلوَ أُخرَى
ويجْهلُ ما المقبلُ؟!

تتنازعُهُ رغباتٌ سواهُ
هو الأوحدُ القحطُ
لا أحدٌ قُربَهُ يهْطِلُ.

كلما نبتَ الأملُ
يترصّدُه منجَلٌ
روحُهُ مسرحٌ أُطفئتْ عنه أضواؤُهُ
وتلاشَى الضجيجُ
وظلَّ يرنُّ صدَى البابِ،
والليلُ في صمتِهِ ههُنا يثملُ.

ولادة
出 生

谢哈·穆泰里 诗人。沙迦大学伊斯兰历史与文明在读博士生，现任朱马·马吉德文化和遗产中心全国文化部主管。著有 5 本诗集，包括《爱的港湾》《我想那是我》等。诗作被译成法、意、葡、俄、西、乌尔都语等。曾获谢哈莎姆萨·宾特·苏海勒创意女性奖、沙迦海湾女性创造力奖等诗歌奖、2019 年"诗人王子"诗歌比赛第二名、金羽毛比赛第一名。2023 年获沙迦阿拉伯诗歌节荣誉诗人称号。

Shaikha Almteiri
谢哈·穆泰里

Shaikha Almteiri (b.1980) is a PhD student in Islamic history and civilization of University of Sharjah. She is the head of national culture department, Juma Almajid Center for Culture and Heritage. She has published five poetry collections, including *Marsa Al-Wedad*, *Lil haneen Baqiyya* and *Ya Akhari wa Kali*. Her poems have been translated into French, Italian, Portuguese, Russian, Urdu and Spanish. She received the Sheikha Shamsa Bint Suhail Award for Creative Women, getting the second in the "Prince of Poets" Competition 2019, the first in Sharjah Award for Gulf Women's Creativity in the Field of Poetry 2022 and the first in the Golden Feather Competition. And she was honored by His Highness Sheikh Dr. Sultan bin Muhammad Al Qasimi to be the honored person at the Sharjah Arab Poetry Festival, January 2023.

出 生

死亡令我忧心
可这生命更让我担忧

我是一张面饼，生在穷人的唇边

我是一把乌德琴，却无人弹唱
我是古老冬季的片刻
焚化在在希望之夏的门前

我出生在穷人的早晨
不记得月份，只知道是夏天
也不知道是何年
虚假的岁月纷纷崩落在这样的事实前：
来者即安，却不会久留

当我出生
哭泣绕着诗歌起舞
我出生在疯子的傍晚
在他们的日子里，我时刻都在出生
没有助产者，没有诗札，没有家庭

我出生了，且仍在出生
我依然独自是所有的问题

（韩誉 译，薛庆国 校译）

ولادة

ويقلقني الموت
لكنّ هذي الحياة تزيد القلق

رغيفاً وحيداً وُلدت على شفة الفقراء

وعُوداً بلا صاحب أو غناء
أنا لحظة من شتاء قديم
على باب صيف الأماني احترق

وُلدتُ صباح المساكين
لا أذكر الشهر لكنه كان صيفاً
ولا أدرك العام
كل السنين تساقطن زيفاً
أمام حقيقة أن يثبت القادمون ولا يثبتون

وُلدتُ
وكان البكاء يدور ويرقص حول القصيدة
وُلدتُ مساء المجانين
وها كنت أولد في يومهم كل حين
بلا قابلة بلا دفتر الشعر والعائلة

وُلدتُ ومازلت أولد
مازلت وحدي هنا الأسئلة

أقول بعيني.. وقلبي بصيرْ..
"我用眼睛说话，我的心无所不见"

阿迈勒·萨赫拉维　诗人，毕业于沙迦大学阿拉伯文学系。现任阿联酋联邦税务总局媒体部主管。代表作有诗集《我不得不推迟你》，广受阿拉伯诗歌读者好评。诗作《时间的奇迹》于 2021 年 7 月通过法拉吉·阿卜耶德的 MET 现场艺术计划在纽约大都会歌剧院成功演出。她曾多次参加国内国际诗歌节，如 2023 年在瓜达拉哈拉举办的墨西哥书展诗歌节等。

Amel Alsahlawi
阿迈勒·萨赫拉维

Amel Alsahlawi (b.1980) is a poet, studied Arabic literature in UOS. She is the Head of Media Section, UAE Federal Tax Authority. Her main works include poetry selection *I had to Postpone You* and lyric *Wonders of Time*. She published her first poetry book in 2020, which was well received by poetry readers in the Arab region. Her poem *Wonders of Time* was successfully performed in the MET - New York through the MET live arts initiative by Faraj Abyad in July 2021. She participated and performed in many poetry events globally and locally such as her most recent international participation in Guadalajara—Mexico Book Fair Poetry Event in 2023.

"我用眼睛说话，我的心无所不见"

我用眼睛说话，我的心无所不见

我的生命与上次的见面等长

我的手是延伸，我的嘴是一口水

我的头脑是床铺，我的灵魂在飞翔

我有一种解脱，热爱永恒

在有爱的同时，我也有一些根源

我有着第一天般的惊奇

我有着疲倦者的厌烦

我的罪孽打磨着我的高傲

我也有着虔诚信徒的醒悟

我有井的干渴、囚徒的焦心

但我并不是那个囚徒

我有早晨的笑声、孩子的快乐

但我并不是那个小孩

明天将喂给我背叛的苹果

但我不会将饥饿廉价出卖

我沉默，仿佛沉默是一种祈祷

在沉默中，全能者听到我的声响

我喜欢在夜之寂静里点亮灯

好让我自己也被照亮

我会这样爱：仿佛你我之间隔着这溪流

而距离恰好是一座桥梁

（韩誉 译，薛庆国 校译）

أقول بعيني.. وقلبي بصيرْ..

أقول بعيني.. وقلبي بصيرْ..
وعمري بطول اللقاء الأخير..
يديّ امتدادٌ.. فمي شربة الماء..
عقلي فراشٌ.. وروحي تطيرْ..
لديّ انعتاقٌ يحبّ الخلود..
لديّ مع الحبّ بعض الجذور..
وبي دهشةٌ مثل أوّل يوم..
وبي ضجر المتعبين الكبيرْ..
تهذّبني في غروري خطاياىَ..
بي صحوة المؤمن المستجير..
وبي عطش البئر.. بي لوعة الأسرِ..
لكنّني.. لستُ ذاك الأسيرْ..
ولي ضحكة الصبح.. بي بهجة الطفل..
لكنّني.. لستُ ذاك الصغير..
ويطعمني الغد تفاحة الغدر..
ما بعتُ جوعي بشيءٍ يسيرْ..
سكتّ كأنّ السكوت صلاةٌ..
ويسمعني.. في السكوت.. القديرْ..
وأحببتُ مثل انبلاج المصابيح
في هدأة الليل.. كي أستنيرْ..
سأهوى كأنّ المسافات جسرٌ..
وبيني وبينك هذا الغدير..

جوان
Молодость
青春 Youth
الشباب जवानी
Juventude

Iran 伊朗

گرداندن

回 归

哈菲兹·阿齐米·卡尔胡兰　诗人，阿尔塔有限责任公司首席执行官。创意写作专业毕业；私人课程工作坊讲师。至今已有 18 年创作经验，著有诗集《可疑的邻居》《强制休假》《食指》等。曾获第六届全国青年诗歌奖第一名和第一届巴哈兰学院诗歌奖一等奖。

Hafez Azimi Kalkhoran
哈菲兹·阿齐米·卡尔胡兰

Hafez Azimi Kalkhoran (b.1988), the Chief Executive Officer of ARTA SHIMI JAM LLC, is a poet with 18 years of writing experience. He is a graduate of creative writing and an instructor of private course workshop. His main works include poetry selections *Suspicious Neighbors*, *Mandatory Leave*, *Hafiz-Khwani*, *Forefinger*, etc. He has won the first place of 6th National Young Poetry Prize and Top Prize of the 1st Baharan Institute Poetry Prize.

回 归

我将以河床的形式回归你
即使你是一条咆哮汹涌的大河
我将以羊群的形式回归你
即使你是一头饥肠辘辘的饿狼
我将以天空的形式回归你
即使你是一片飘忽不定的云朵

然而，你的双腿，已经是现代的双腿
对大自然已经了无记忆
对我这样的一个红皮肤人已经了无记忆
即使是用烟囱的烟雾也无法
让双腿明白
回归的涵义

（穆宏燕 译）

گرداندن

باز می گرداندمت به بستر

حتی رودی طغیانگر اگر بودی

باز می گرداندمت به گله

حتی گرگی گرسنه اگر بودی

باز می گرداندمت به آسمان

حتی ابری گریزان اگر بودی

پاهای تو اما پاهایی مدرن اند

بی هیچ تعلق خاطری به طبیعت

بی هیچ تعلق خاطری به یک سرخ پوست چون من

که حتی با دود سیگارش هم نمی تواند

به آن ها بفهماند

مفهوم بازگشت را

سلول انفرادی
单人牢房

基亚努什·汉·穆罕默迪　诗人、剧作家、导演。设计专业硕士，现任日诺拉设计工作室高级产品设计师。著有诗集《十，十分钟和三十秒》《石头跳出溺水的恐惧》等。曾获第一届全国尼亚瓦兰诗歌节奖、第四届扎格罗斯诗歌节奖、第一届沙姆赛诗歌节奖等奖项。作品被译成英、西、阿、土等语言。

Kianoosh Khan Mohammadi
基亚努什·汉·穆罕默迪

Kianoosh Khan Mohammadi (b.1985), the Senior Product Designer of Zhinoora Design Studio with a Master's degree in product design, is a poet and playwright. His main works include poetry selections *Ten*, *Ten Minutes and Thirty Seconds* and *The Stones Jump from the Fear of Drowning*, etc. He was awarded Annual Book of Poetry of the Journalists Annual Book, the 1st Niavaran National Poetry Festival Prize, the 1st Shamseh Poetry Festival Prize and 4th National Zagros Poetry Festival Prize. His works have been translated into English, Spanish, Arabic, Turkish, etc.

单人牢房

狱卒说：单人牢房是死亡的兄弟，比死亡更无情
它把它的牺牲从这个世界带走却不送到另一个世界
狱卒对空空的单人牢房很恐惧
因为在单人牢房中总是会有人在
即使没有人，牢房里的空气也会凝聚出一个轮廓
悲伤的容积
没有人却在牢房中游走
没有人但它的头会撞击牢房的墙壁
没有人甚至连这些都没有，只有孤独
狱卒不明白
那个老囚犯在牢房沿墙根走动，哭泣
用头撞击墙壁却不说话
多年以来早已逃脱！

（穆宏燕 译）

سلول انفرادی

زندانبان گفت: «سلول انفرادی برادر مرگ است، اما بی رحم تر!

او قربانیانش را از این جهان می گیرد اما به جهان دیگر نمی بَرد!»

زندانبان از سلول های انفرادی خالی می ترسد

چون در سلول های انفرادی همیشه کسی هست

حتی وقتی هم که کسی نیست، هوای سلول، حجمی به اندازه یک انسان را در خود خالی نگه میدارد

حجمی غمگین،

که نیست اما در سلول راه میرود

نیست اما در سلول گریه میکند

نیست اما سرش را به دیوار سلول میکوبد

نیست اما حتی با وجود اینکه نیست، تنهاست

زندانبان نمی فهمد

آن زندانی پیر که سالهاست در سلول کناری راه میرود، گریه میکند،

و سرش را به دیوار میکوبد اما حرف نمیزند،

سالهاست گریخته!

سیب
苹 果

伊德里斯·巴赫蒂亚里 诗人。国际大学历史学硕士，现就职于《沙赫拉拉报》。25 岁开始创作。著有诗集《马鲁斯山谷》《耶路撒冷之歌》。曾获图斯诗歌节一等奖、二等奖，2016 年获沙姆卢奖提名。

Edrees Bakhtiari
伊德里斯·巴赫蒂亚里

Edrees Bakhtiari (b.1982), serving in Shahrara Newspaper with a Master's degree in history, is a poet who started writing at the age of 25. He is the author of poetry selections *Marus Valley* and *Songs of Jerusalem*. Nominee for Shamlu's Literature Award, he has got first and second prize in National Festival of Toos at Neyshabur.

苹 果

我把一根树枝拽向我自己这边

采摘上面的苹果

悬吊着的苹果

简直就如同一只牛眼盯着我

我在家乡的时候

苹果园常说

你是弯曲的树枝上最后剩下的果实

你的血是苹果

你的唇是苹果

你的酒是苹果

你躺在我的树枝上，睡我的苹果

苹果树，衰老了

当我从那上面离开

却见我也衰老了，竟不知苹果的名字

我只好让大家囫囵吞下

以便能创造出另外三个字母*

跌落在我的衣裙上

---

* 波斯语中，"苹果（sīb）"一词是由三个字母组成的。

سیب

یک شاخه را کشیدم سمت خودم

و از آن سیب ها را چیدم

سیب هایی که معلق بودند

درست عین گاو یک چشم نگاهم کردند

من در زادگاهم بودم

و باغ سیب می گفت

تو آخرین بازمانده از درختان خم شده ای

خونت سیب

لبت سیب

شرابت سیب

بر شاخه ام دراز می کشی و می خوابی سیب ام

درخت سیب ، پیر شد

تا از آن بالا رفتم

دیدم پیرم و اسم سیب ها را نمی دانم

گذاشتم قل بخورند

تا سه حرف دیگر بسازند

افتاند در دامنم

只见我吃了苹果

吃了苹果树

因为我根本就不看它们

我吃了我的梦

你若结实就好了

你若成苹果就好了

你若成熟就好了

你若飘荡就好了

你若坠落就好了

——我在梦中

（穆宏燕 译）

دیدم سیب ها را خورده ام

درخت ها را خورده ام

چون آن ها را نمی بینم

خوابم را خورده ام

کاش می آمدی

سیب می شدی

می رسیدی

سبک می شدی

می افتادی

ـــ در خوابم

روح رفته
出走的灵魂

لحظه
一　瞬

卡齐姆·瓦埃兹扎德　诗人、评论家，萨伯林出版社销售经理。波斯文学硕士。著有诗集《一瞥之雨》《黑暗翻译》《风的延续》《流水归河》《私人历史》等。自 2006 年起教授诗歌创作，建立伊朗第一所专业诗歌学院，成立诗歌文学协会，组织多个诗歌工作坊，担任朱梅节等诗歌节评委。在多个文学期刊上发表文章。

青春，如风有信

Kazem Vaezzadeh
卡齐姆·瓦埃兹扎德

Kazem Vaezzadeh (b.1981) is the sales manager of Saberin Publication and a poet teaching poetry and editor of poetry workshops since 2006. Establishing Sepid Age Literary Association and School of Poetry, the first academy specially for poetry in Iran, he was the judge of Giume Poetry Festival. His main works include poetry selections *The Rain of Glance*, *Translation of Darkness*, *Along the Winds*, *The Lost Waters Return to the River*, *Dawdling*, *Private History*, etc. His articles were published in lots of literary journals.

出走的灵魂

出走的灵魂
试图回归原本的肉体
非为旧日遗忘的言语
也非为我对你的爱
只为窗边的那只花瓶
为在另一世界
未找寻到的东西

一　瞬

我的祖先们
划分了昼夜
　　　　同等的时间
都化为一瞬连一瞬
他们未曾见过你
他们不曾知晓
这一路的漫长与凛冽
也不知你缺席了几分几秒

（阳融寒 译）

روح رفته

روح رفته
می کوشد به تن برگردد
نه برای گفتن حرفی که فراموش شده
نه برای دوستت دارم
تنها برای گلدانی کنار پنجره
چیزی که در جهان دیگر
پیدا نکرده است.

لحظه

اجدادم
شبانه روز را تقسیم کردند
ساعت های برابر
به لحظه ها و
آنها تو را ندیده بودند
نمی دانستند
چه قدر میتواند طولانی و سرد باشد
دقیقه های نبودنت.

وقتی همه نامردند
当大家都不仗义

穆罕默德·侯赛因·巴赫拉米扬　诗人，大学教授。毕业于设拉子大学波斯语言文学系，曾任教于法尔斯省多所大学。著有多种著述，包括诗集《这些补丁不适合月亮》《我的情人曾是所有单词》《比任何偶然都更是常态》等。文章散见于各报纸刊物。曾获得阿扎德大学全国奥米德诗歌节冠军，入选第 22 届伊朗波斯语图书周法尔斯省最受读者欢迎的作者。

Mohammad Hossein Bahramian
穆罕默德·侯赛因·巴赫拉米扬

Mohammad Hossein Bahramian (b.1969), graduated from the Department of Farsi Language and Literature of Shiraz University, has been teaching in many universities of Fars Province. His main works include poetry selections *In Vasleha be Mah Nemichasbid*, *Ma 'shugheha-yi Man Hame Kaleme Budand*, *Hamishe-tar az Har Che Etfagh*, etc. His articles have been published in various journals and magazines. He is the winner of the National Omid Poetry Festival of Islamic Azad University and is the best book author of the 22nd Iran-Persian Book Week in Fars Province.

当大家都不仗义

姑娘! 你千万不要想投湖自尽

那水比你身子受到的玷污更肮脏

你的被玷污是一种美丽

在身体之茧中憧憬着变成飞蛾吧

花儿总是会枯黄, 男人们全都是铁石心肠

当大家都不仗义, 是爱让你成为女人

佐列哈的伤害啊! 手掌沉浸在血泊中啊!

但愿我身体的骚动能被家乡拥抱

尽管我知道优素福

被我衣衫之黑夜监狱的名声侵害 *

我的灵魂伴随着一声叹息, 从存在中长出翅膀

你是精神, 我担心你做了身体的羁绊

我语言的容颜与你同在, 沉默的镜子啊!

尽管我没有看见你有讲话的渴望

那就把想从自己发出的呐喊和怒吼都扔掉吧

成为一道闪电, 做暴风雨, 击碎惊涛骇浪

佛陀的莲花, 你不是水洼, 而是大海

可惜啊你被一摊淤泥羁绊

(穆宏燕 译)

---

* 这里乃用《古兰经》中的典故。优素福被卖到埃及后, 在埃及大臣家做奴仆。大臣的妻子佐列哈爱上了英俊貌美的优素福。一次, 佐列哈把优素福带到内室想与之亲近, 优素福逃离。两人在拉扯之中, 优素福的衣衫被佐列哈撕裂。佐列哈在大臣面前诬告优素福调戏她。该诗中的"我"指佐列哈。在波斯诗人

وقتی همه نامردند

بانو! نکند فکرِ مرداب شدن باشی

آبی تر از آنی که آلوده ی تن باشی

تو سوختنت زیباست، انگار خدا می خواست

در پیله ی تن گرمِ پروانه شدن باشی

گلها همگی زردند، مردان همه بی دردند

وقتی همه نامردند، عشق است که زن باشی

ای زخم زلیخایی! ای چنگ فرو در خون!

آشوبِ تنم را کاش آغوشِ وطن باشی

هر چند که می دانم یوسف تر از آنی که

زندانیِ شب های پیراهنِ من باشی

من روحم و با یک آه، پر می کشم از بودن

تو جانی و می ترسم پابندِ بدن باشی

رویِ سخنم با توست ای آینه خاموش!

هر چند نمی بینم مشتاق سخن باشی

بشکن که برانگیزی فریاد و فغان از خویش

رعدی شو و طوفان باش تا موج شکن باشی

نیلوفر بودایی، تو برکه نه، دریایی

حیف است گرفتارِ یک مشت لجن باشی

（接上页）贾米（1414—1492）创作的长篇爱情叙事诗《优素福与佐列哈》中，佐列哈最后获得精神的洗礼，与优素福终成眷属。该诗也是运用了佐列哈"浴火重生"的典故。

The Charge
指 控

阿里-礼萨·加兹韦赫 著名诗人，伊朗诗歌和音乐广播电视中心主任。塔吉克斯坦大学语言学博士。著有多部诗集，荣获多个国家级文学奖项，执导过多个诗歌音乐节。诗歌被翻译成多个语种出版。

Alireza Ghazveh
阿里-礼萨·加兹韦赫

Alireza Ghazveh (b.1964), serving as the Director of the Radio and Television Center for Poetry and Music of Iran, is an eminent Iranian poet with a doctor's degree in philology. He is the author of many poetry selections of various topics and the winner of different national literary awards, and he has directed several poetry festivals. His works have been translated into many foreign languages.

指 控

苹果树被传唤
戴上手铐
指控是
……它像扔石头一样, 扔它的果实!
橘子树被传唤
指控是
它今年的果实是血淋淋的! ……
橄榄树被传唤
指控是
……它把所有其他果实都生成了子弹!
全体起立! 法庭正在开庭
被告是被命令停止的一波海浪
但它没有停止!
被告是一只鸽子,
它没有离开锡安!
被告是一只麻雀,
它不懂希伯来语!
法庭正在开庭
被告是知识之树 (那知善恶的)
和通往天堂的阶梯!
被告是所有那些墓碑
上面刻着"真主"的名字
和所有那些母亲
在她们的子宫里,
生下的孩子
手里拿着石头!

(赵四 译)

The Charge

The Apple tree is summoned
In cuffs
The charge is that
… It has thrown its fruits; like stone!
The Orange tree is summoned
The charge is that
Its fruits are bloody this year!…
The Olive tree is summoned
The charge is that
… It has born bullets every other fruit!
All Rise! The court is in session
The Respondent is a Wave who has been ordered to STOP
And it has not!
Respondent is a Dove,
Who did not leave Zion!
Respondent is a Sparrow,
Who knows no Hebrew!
The court is in session
Respondent is the tree of knowledge (of good and bad)
And the Ladder to the Heavens!
The Respondents are all those gravestones
With the name of 'Allah' on them
And all those mothers
Who in their wombs,
Bear children that
Hold stone in hand!

جوان
Молодость
青春 Youth
جوانी الشباب
Juventude

埃塞俄比亚

Ethiopia

Apocalypse
启示录

费本·方乔　诗人、文学活动家，精神科住院医师。毕业于季马大学医学院，现就读于圣保罗千禧医学院精神病学硕士专业。作为诗歌平台"吉特赛腾"经理，主持过多场诗歌朗诵，参与过亚的斯亚贝巴诗歌节等活动的组织工作。

Feben Fancho
费本·方乔

Feben Fancho (b.1992), a psychiatry resident doctor, is a poet and literary activist. Graduated from Jimma University Medical College, she is now a student pursuing an MA degree of psychiatry in Saint Paul's Hospital Millennium Medical College. As the general manager of Gitem Sitem, she has hosted many open mic poetry stages, being a part of organizing national poetry festival in Addis Ababa.

启示录

如果我们是地球上最后行走的人

最后灭亡的人

在审判日还继续奔跑的人

当火从天上如雨而降

我仍会以我的身体紧贴你的身体

努力尝试

以汗水和精液灭火

而当我的皮肤融化

我的子宫还会

承接你的种子和信仰

我会抚养我们的孩子

即使身在地狱

（范静哗 译）

Apocalypse

If we were the last to walk on earth

The last to perish

And keep running on the day of judgement

Where fire rains from the heavens

I will still keep my body glued to yours

And try to put off the fire

Using sweat and semen

And while my skin melts

My uterus will conceive

Your seed and believe

I will raise our kids

Even in hell

Finding Yourself?
寻找自己?

策加耶·吉尔梅　诗人、译者。毕业于亚的斯亚贝巴大学外语系英语专业,副修法语专业,以优异成绩取得对外英语教学硕士学位。曾在亚的斯亚贝巴大学英语系教授英文写作。2016 年出版首部诗歌散文集。

Tsegaye Hailesilassie Girmay
策加耶·吉尔梅

Tsegaye Hailesilassie Girmay (b.1989) is a poet, translator and essayist, graduated from Addis Ababa University in foreign languages and literature with an English major and a French minor. He has completed MA courses in Teaching English as a Foreign Language (TEFL). He taught at the English Department of Addis Ababa University with a focus on English writing courses. In 2016, he published his first book of poetry and essays.

寻找自己?

旅行从不是寻找自己。你永远找不到。

怎么能找到你自己呢?
"自我"从未创造出来,
甚至还没开始创造。
而你,每个特定时刻都完整无缺,
不还是总在破立之中?

所以,
或许,
你该放下心来,
明白你没有必要为了找到自己,
必须走什么的路,
必须解什么的谜!

（范静哗 译）

Finding Yourself?

The journey is not to find yourself; you never will.

How could you find you?
When 'self' is never made,
Or not even in the making?
When you, being fully whole at every moment,
Are nonetheless always breaking?

So
May be
You should be at rest
Knowing there is no road you need to travel,
No mystery you ought to unravel,
To find you!

... to reborn

……重生

塞费·泰曼　诗人、教育者、文学活动家。诗歌平台"吉特赛腾"创始人、总经理，诗歌朗诵活动"诗意星期六"常驻诗人，"非洲砸诗杯"形象大使。获得 2021 年埃塞俄比亚全国砸诗大赛冠军。

Seife Temam
塞费·泰曼

Seife Temam (b.1988) is a poet, educator and literary activist. He is the founder and manager of Gitem Sitem, a poetry platform representing Ethiopia in World Poetry Slam Organization, and senior copywriter of Zeleman. Also he is a resident poet of literary event Poetic Saturdays, the ambassador for Cup of African Slam Poetry. He won the Ethiopian National Slam Champion in 2021.

……重生

我们分开很久了

我们挡住了道路, 为了建设自己那一部分

那一部分本该

使我们所有人解脱

一个部分永远属于我们, 一个部分永远失去……

那时, 我们的心圆滑

没有人可在上面行走或停留

我们的宽恕被冲刷一尽

连同我们的美德和表达自己意见的机会

我们剩下的只是一串互相绑缚

一串渲染粉饰和各种腐朽

我们这些无敌的人类同胞有祸了

那看不见的从内而外地杀死了我们

所以, 让我们不要挡住任何道路

即便它通向地狱

我们的善行和善意

将是唯一可说的

让我们忠于我们和他人身上的纽带

以非血肉的心灵, 让我们重新结合以获重生!

(赵四 译)

... to reborn

For ages, we've been apart

We blocked the road to build a part

A part that was supposed

to disentangle us all

A part forever ours, a part forever lost ...

Back then, our hearts were slickery

For no one to walk or stay

Our forgiveness was all washed away

With our virtue and our chance to have our say

What's left of us is a string of bonds

A string of colors and all sorts of a decay

Woe to us for the invincible fellow humans we are

And the invisible killing us from inside out

So, let's not block any road

Even if it leads to hell

Our good deeds and our goodwill

Will be the only thing left to tell

Let's stick to the strings that are in us and in others

With a fleshless mind, let's re-bond to reborn!

جوان
Молодость
青春 Youth
الشباب जवानी
Juventude

China 中国

The Chinese Courier
中国快递员

王二冬 1990 年生于山东无棣，新工业代表诗人、山东省作协签约作家，快递行业从业者。著有诗集《快递中国》《东河西营》等多种。曾获第四届草堂诗歌奖"年度诗人奖"，第三届中国红高粱诗歌奖、第三十届樱花诗歌奖等，参加《诗刊》社第 36 届青春诗会。

王二冬
Wang Erdong

Wang Erdong (b.1990) was born in Wudi, Shandong Province. He is a poet who writes about new industrial developments and is a writer under contract to the Shandong Provincial Writers Association. He is also employed in the express delivery market. He has published several poetry collections including *Express China* and *The Village of Donghe Xiying*. Wang was awarded the "Poet of the Year" of the 4th Thatched Cottage Poetry Award and has been the recipient of the 3rd Red Sorghum Poetry Award and the 30th Cherry Blossom Poetry Award. He has participated in the 36th Young Poets' Meeting organized by the *Poetry Periodical*.

中国快递员

他们的名字
值得站在一首诗的顶峰
感受高处的雪和阳光
包裹正抓着一丝亮
向上攀登

这是用快件堆起的山
他们独自上山、下山
又在深夜把最后一块石头
刨掉，沉睡中
他们绷紧的身体
才会跌落进溪谷

梦中，他们仍一遍遍
念着别人的名字
却从未提起自己叫什么
如果年轻，就被称为快递小哥
如果脚步渐缓
就被喊作老张、老王

The Chinese Courier

Their names
Deserve to be chanted as the climax of a poem
Glorious as snow and sunlight on a mountain peak
Clutching their parcels of light
They clamber upwards

Over the mountains of mail
They wend their solitary ways
Working through the darkest nights,
They shift the final stones
Only in slumber
Will their tense bodies
Gently fall in soothing hollows

In dreams they still pronounce
The names of others
Yet never mention their own
The young are known as 'the delivery boy'
As you get older you'll be called
'Uncle Zhang' or 'Uncle Wang'

——呵，无名之辈

我们身边最熟悉的人

如果一个快件高半米

一个快递员每天配送一百五十件

每年可以堆起三座珠穆朗玛峰

他们的名字值得被刻在上面

因此，我从不吝惜

把最宏大的词用在最普通的人身上

他们默默做着最微小的事

很少被夸赞，更不会自夸

他们的习以为常

在日复一日的奔波中

已足够伟大

—Oh, nameless ones!

Our most familiar visitors

If a parcel is half a meter tall

And 150 are delivered every day

Then three Mount Everests could be constructed every year

And their names should be engraved on each one

Therefore I never hesitate to apply

The grandest words to the most ordinary of people

Quietly they do the smallest things

Seldom praised, and never boastful

They plod on with their work unceasingly

Every single day and this to me

Is a form of greatness

（彼得·休斯、黄心怡 译）

Fireworks
焰 火

马骥文 1990 年生，回族。清华大学文学博士，现供职于青海民族大学，出版有诗集《妙体》《唯一与感知者》，曾获十月诗歌奖、草堂诗歌奖、未名诗歌奖等奖项。

马骥文
Ma Jiwen

Ma Jiwen (b.1990) is of Hui ethnicity and currently resides in Xi'ning. He holds a PhD in literature from Tsinghua University and is employed at Qinghai Minzu University. His published poetry collections include *The Mystical Body* and *The Only and the Perceiver*. He has received numerous accolades, including the *October* Poetry Award, the Thatched Cottage Poetry Award, and the Weiming Poetry Award.

焰 火

美使我们合为一个。傍晚的爱人
拥抱在辽阔的星空下, 将夜的余温
降临给对方。四月之火, 在暗暗的
传递中发出年月般持久的光柱
并提升着他们中的每一个
似乎, 唯有寂静才能让我们变得洁白
你注视那瞬间的事物, 迷人的碎裂
正把更深的爱引入你的手中, 如狂泻之雪
而什么是抵达? 不可能的才是真实
除了你, 在颤动、节制与熄灭中
照亮我的将属于另一种完美的例外
此刻, 飞旋如命的火花
在空气中涌聚着你我的激荡与消亡
可它仍是美感, 与每一个被它所引照的人
交换着最终来临的形式和词语
在瀑布般的未来闪现为诗人的荣耀

Fireworks

Beauty unites us. Evening lovers kiss beneath a star-filled sky

Gifting each other the night's last warmth

The fire of April passes through the darkness

In columns of light as long as the years,

Raising every year into the heavens.

It seems that only silence can restore us.

You observe that fleeting moment, sweet fragmentation

Bringing deeper love into your hands, like torrential snow.

And what is arrival? The impossible is what is real.

Except for you, in the trembling moderations and extinctions,

The one who brightens me will also be unique.

At this moment, the sparks fly up like life

Gathering our excitement and our endings into air.

Yet it is beauty still, exchanging final forms and words

With each illuminated soul flashing

In the cascades of the future as a poet's glory.

（彼得·休斯、安文婧 译）

Replacing the Tile
补瓦记

王单单　原名王丹，1982 年生，云南镇雄人。现供职于云南省文联。出版诗集《山冈诗稿》《春山空》《花鹿坪手记》、随笔集《借人间避雨》等。曾获《人民文学》新人奖、《诗刊》年度青年诗人奖、华文青年诗人奖、扬子江青年诗人奖、艾青诗歌奖、云南文学艺术奖等。系第 13 届首都师范大学驻校诗人。《钟山》《扬子江文学评论》"新世纪二十年青年诗人 20 家"，2020 年中国作协"深入生活、扎根人民"主题实践先进个人。

王单单
Wang Dandan

Wang Dandan (b.1982) was born in Zhenxiong, Yunnan Province. He currently works at the Yunnan Provincial Writers Association. He has published poetry collections such as *The Manuscripts of Mountain Ridge Poems*, *Empty Spring Mountains*, *Handwritten Notes in Hualuping Village*, and essay collections including *Sheltering from the Rain in the Human World*. Wang Dandan has received many accolades, including the *People's Literature* Newcomer Award, the Young Poet of the Year by the *Poetry Periodical*, the Chinese Young Poets Award, the Yangtze River Annual Award for Young Poets, the Ai Qing Poetry Award, and the Yunnan Literature and Art Award. He served as the 13th Resident Poet at Capital Normal University, and was recognized as one of the "20 Young Poets of the New Century" by *Zhongshan* magazine and *The Yangtze River Literature Reviews*.

补瓦记

秋后的原野上
一个人奔跑在雨水之前
他要赶去对面的山崖下
为阿金家的屋顶补一片瓦——
一片亮瓦啊，这方寸之地
可纳浩瀚星空，就像人的眼睛
面对着世间的深邃

阿金站在屋里，仰头
指挥着屋顶上盖瓦的人
"向左一些，朝右一点……"
隔着巴掌大的亮瓦
阿金看到它背面，有一张
脸，流汗的脸——
从容，坚毅，大如天

Replacing the Tile

Across the autumn field
A man runs ahead of the rain.
Rushing to reach the far ridge
To fix a tile on Ajin's roof –
A shiny tile, a tiny gap
Containing the great starry sky, like an eye
Facing the depths of the world.

Ajin stands inside looking up
Guiding the roofer.
'Left a bit, slightly to the right...'
Through the palm-sized opening
Ajin sees an absence of tile
He sees a sweaty face
Calm, determined, big as the sky.

（彼得·休斯、安文婧 译）

Moon on the Canal
运河里的月亮

方石英　1980 年生，浙江台州人，现居杭州，中国作家协会会员。著有诗集《独自摇滚》《石头诗》《运河里的月亮》《漂泊的石头》等。作品入选《〈诗刊〉创刊 60 周年诗选》《新中国 70 年优秀文学作品文库·诗歌卷》等选本。曾获第十五届"华文青年诗人奖"、浙江省优秀文学作品奖、浙江省"新荷计划·实力作家奖"等奖项。参加《诗刊》社第 32 届"青春诗会"、鲁迅文学院第 34 届高研班。

方石英
Fang Shiying

Fang Shiying (b.1980) was born in Taizhou, Zhejiang Province, and currently resides in Hangzhou. He is a member of the China Writers Association. He has published poetry collections such as *Rocking Alone*, *The Poetry of the Stone*, *Moon on the Canal* and *Drifting Stones*. His works have been included in anthologies like *The 60th Anniversary Anthology of the Poetry Periodical* and *The 70 Years of New China's Outstanding Literary Works: Poetry Volume*. He has received awards including the 15th Chinese Young Poets Award, the Award for Outstanding Literary Works in Zhejiang, and the Zhejiang Province's New Lotus Plan: Outstanding Writer Award. He also participated in the 32nd Young Poets' Meeting held by the *Poetry Periodical* and the 34th advanced training program of Lu Xun Literature Academy.

运河里的月亮

多少次我是一张洁白的宣纸
在暮色中，依靠微弱的霞光
静静飘落水面
我的每一个毛孔都在倾听
流水，一场尚未命名的恋爱
等着月亮升起来

我宣布，我终于失败了
在充满鱼腥味的空气中
有从树木年轮里渗出的忧伤
哦，回忆需要一个起点，而终点
是运河里的月亮，长着一张多变的脸
一张让我痛哭之后依然想哭的脸

我宣布，我终于失败了
即使烂醉如泥
也无法挽回，各个朝代的瓷片
在水底一起尖叫
而我的月亮，运河里的月亮
是一场梦，开始流向我儿子

Moon on the Canal

Time and time again, I'm a blank piece
of Xuan paper, quietly falling on the water
in the faint evening glow.
Every pore on my skin listens
as the water flows by, an unnamed love
awaiting the moonrise.

I declare total failure, finally.
In the fishy air I smell sadness
that permeates through the wood's rings.
O, memory requires a beginning, but the endpoint is the moon
in the canal, whose face is always changing,
a face that makes me cry after my tears dry out.

Finally, I have to admit failure,
a failure with no redemption even if I get stewed
to the gills. Fragments of porcelain from past dynasties
are shrieking in the river bed
and my moon, drifting on the canal,
is a dream that flows down to my son.

（阿九 译）

Aili Kram's Horse
艾力·克拉姆的马

卢山 1987 年生于安徽宿州,新疆阿拉尔市作协主席,浙江省作协诗歌委员会委员。出版有《宝石山居图》《将雪推回天山》等四本诗集,印有评论集《我们时代的诗青年》,主编(合作)《新湖畔诗选》《野火诗丛》《江南风度:21 世纪杭嘉湖诗选》等。参加《诗刊》社第 38 届青春诗会、第 12 届十月诗会等。

卢山
Lu Shan

Lu Shan (b.1987) was born in Suzhou, Anhui Province. He is the President of the Aral Municipal Writers Association in Xinjiang Uygur Autonomous Region and a member of the Poetry Committee of the Zhejiang Provincial Writers Association. His published works include poetry collections *Dwelling in the Baoshi Mountains* and *Pushing Snow Back to Tianshan Mountains*, and a critical essay collection *Young Poets of Our Time*. He was the Editor-in-Chief for anthologies such as *New Lakeside Poetry Selection* (with other editors), *Wildfire Poetry Series*, and *Elegance of Jiangnan: A Selection of 21st Century Poetry*. He participated in the 38th Young Poets' Meeting held by the *Poetry Periodical* and the 12th *October* magazine's Poetry Conference.

艾力·克拉姆的马

在博孜墩草原，黄昏时
我看见一匹老马一瘸一拐地
从树林里走出来
身上挂着柴草和荆棘
时不时地跌倒在土坑旁
它的眼神充满晚秋的忧伤
警觉又无奈地望着我

它的后腿张开血红的伤口
里面还残留着几根尖叫的铁丝
像一个暮年的老兵
它曾经跨越千山万水
如今蹒跚垂首
黄昏的光线催促它
缓慢地走向一个篱笆

艾力·克拉姆端来一盆水
清洗它的脊背。拍了拍老马的头
像是在问候他的伙计
他嘴里说着我听不懂的话语
用手梳理那些打结的鬃毛
老马把头埋进他脏兮兮的怀里
温顺地发出阵阵叹息
不远处的烟囱升起炊烟
雪山逐渐隐匿在黄昏里

Aili Kram's Horse

At dusk on the Bosidun prairie,
I saw an old horse limp out of the woods
Its coat snagged with sticks and thorns,
Sometimes stumbling on the uneven ground.
Its eyes were filled with late autumn sadness,
It watched me with cautious helplessness.

Its hind legs showed bloody wounds
Still trapped by vicious barbs of wire.
Like an ageing soldier it had crossed
A thousand mountains and rivers,
But now staggered with a bowed head.
The twilight urged it onwards
Slowly toward a fence.

Aili Kram brought a basin of water
To wash its back. He patted the old horse's head,
As if greeting an old comrade,
Mumbling words I didn't understand
He combed out the tangled mane.
The old horse buried its head in his dirty embrace,
Gently sighing.
Smoke rose from a chimney, not far away.
The snow-capped mountains gradually faded in the dusk.

（彼得·休斯、安文婧 译）

Seeking Cranes
寻 鹤

冯娜 1985 年生于云南丽江，白族。一级作家、诗人，毕业并任职于中山大学。著有《无数灯火选中的夜》《寻鹤》等诗文集、译著十余部，参加《诗刊》社第 29 届青春诗会。首都师范大学第十二届驻校诗人。曾获中国少数民族骏马奖、华文青年诗人奖等文学奖项。作品被翻译成英、俄、日、韩语等译介到海外。

冯娜
Feng Na

Feng Na (b.1985) was born in Lijiang, Yunnan Province, and is of Bai ethnicity. A writer and poet, she graduated from and now works at Sun Yat-sen University. She has authored over 10 poetry collections and translations such as *Nights Chosen by Countless Lights* and *Seeking Cranes*. She participated in the 29th Young Poets' Meeting organized by the *Poetry Periodical* and served as the 12th Resident Poet at Capital Normal University. Feng Na has received multiple literary awards including the Fine Horse Prize for National Ethnic Literary Creation and the Chinese Young Poets Award. Her works have been translated into many languages including English, Russian, Japanese, and Korean.

寻 鹤

牛羊藏在草原的阴影中
巴音布鲁克 我遇见一个养鹤的人
他有长喙一般的脖颈
断翅一般的腔调
鹤群掏空落在水面的九个太阳
他让我觉得草原应该另有模样

黄昏轻易纵容了辽阔
我等待着鹤群从他的袍袖中飞起
我祈愿天空落下另一个我
她有狭窄的脸庞 瘦细的脚踝
与养鹤人相爱 厌弃 痴缠
四野茫茫 她有一百零八种躲藏的途径
养鹤人只需一种寻找的方法：
在巴音布鲁克
被他抚摸过的鹤 都必将在夜里归巢

Seeking Cranes

Cattle and sheep hide in the grassland's shadows.

In Bayanbulak I met a man who cared for cranes,

He had a beak-like neck,

And a tone as broken as clipped wings.

The cranes hollowed out the nine suns that fell into the water,

He made me feel the grasslands should look different.

Dusk easily indulges the vastness,

I wait for the cranes to take wing from his sleeves,

I pray for another self to descend from the sky,

She has a slim face and slender ankles,

She loves, rejects, and is obsessed with the keeper of cranes.

In the vast wilderness she has a hundred and eight hiding places,

The crane keeper needs just a single way to find her:

In Bayanbulak

The cranes he has touched will return to their nests at night.

（彼得·休斯、安文婧 译）

Harvest
收 获

吕周杭 2000 年生，现就读于吉林大学。即将出版诗集《松鼠记》，曾获《诗刊》2022 陈子昂年度青年诗人奖，2023 东荡子诗歌奖·高校奖。参加《诗刊》社第 39 届青春诗会。

吕周杭
Lü Zhouhang

Lü Zhouhang (b.2000) is currently studying at Jilin University. His poetry collection *Memoirs of a Squirrel* will soon be published. Lü has received the 2022 Chen Zi'ang Young Poet of the Year Award from the *Poetry Periodical* and the 2023 Dong Dangzi Poetry Award for College Students. He participated in the 39th Young Poets' Meeting organized by the *Poetry Periodical*.

收 获

十月的光线在外部劳作
尘土发烫，声音通过振动联结彼此

在十月的玻璃房，她小心翼翼地旋转，挪腾
太阳像一颗笨重的蟹钳摇摇欲坠

果实在传递。幸福在分享中得到形状
所有的目击者都信誓旦旦

我们握着春天的树对秋天的信心
尝试理解，就像风雨也曾徙经我们的躯干

Harvest

October sunlight is doing its work,
The dust is hot, the sounds connected through vibration.

In the greenhouse, she cautiously manoeuvers.
The sun is like a heavy crab claw just about to fall.

Fruit is passed on. Happiness forms through sharing,
All the witnesses make their vows.

We maintain the spring tree's confidence in autumn,
We try to understand, just as the wind and rain
Have also passed throughout our trunks and branches.

（彼得·休斯、黄心怡 译）

A Small Town Tale
小城故事

年微漾　1988 年生，福建仙游人，著有诗集《扫雪记》等三种，获柔刚诗歌奖、丁玲文学奖等，参加鲁迅文学院第 34 期高研班、《诗刊》社第 35 届青春诗会。

年微漾
Nian Weiyang

Nian Weiyang (b.1988) was born in Xianyou, Fujian Province. He has authored three poetry collections including *Snow Sweeping Chronicle*, and has received the Rougang Poetry Award and the Ding Ling Literature Award. He also participated in the 34th advanced training program of Lu Xun Literature Academy and the 35th Young Poets' Meeting organized by the *Poetry Periodical*.

小城故事

大体是平静的：榕树的浓荫
覆盖公路。偶有汽车开过
带来转瞬即逝的幻想

从西河到四桥，有段废弃已久的江面
夜里，船只屈指可数
仿佛正熨着一件发皱的纪念品

是的，礼物有时替我们说出
难以启齿的感情。一件布偶、一块石头
或一只铁罐，都是来自身上的器官

那年十月，三角梅凋谢
城中小小的房屋，窗户向北
没有可供发愁的明天
你站在巷口简短告别
巷子里有家杂货铺
女店主靠生火捱过寒冬

小火炉上火焰在跳舞
我也想有这样的妻子
她爱这个家爱得噼啪作响

A Small Town Tale

The gentle shade of banyan trees
Covers the road. Occasionally a car goes by
Bringing one more fleeting dream.

From Xihe to Siqiao there drifts
A long-abandoned stretch of river
At night there are just a few ships,
That seem to iron out a wrinkled souvenir.

Sometimes a gift can speak for us,
Putting hidden feelings into words. A doll, a stone,
A tin – each can bring a message from within.

That October, the bougainvillea withered,
A small house with north-facing windows,
There were no worries left for tomorrow.
You stood in the alley to say a quick goodbye,
There was a grocery store there, the shopkeeper
Keeping out the cold by tending a small fire.

Flames are dancing on the little stove,
I too wished for such a wife,
To love this home with such a dancing warmth.

（彼得·休斯、安文婧 译）

Riding Whales
骑鲸记

刘康　1989 年生，江苏常州人，出版诗集《骑鲸记》《万象》，获紫金山文学奖、《钟山》之星文学奖、扬子江青年诗人奖等，《骑鲸记》入选 21 世纪文学之星丛书（2020 卷）。参加《诗刊》社第 37 届青春诗会。

刘康
Liu Kang

Liu Kang (b.1989) was born in Changzhou, Jiangsu Province. His published poetry collections include *Riding Whales* and *Ten Thousand Things*. Liu Kang has received accolades such as the Purple Mountain Literature Award, the Star of *Zhongshan* magazine Literature Award, and the Yangtze River Annual Award for Young Poets. *Riding Whales* was included in the *Star of 21st Century Literature Series* (2020). He also participated in the 37th Young Poets' Meeting organized by the *Poetry Periodical*.

骑鲸记

大海的栅栏随波涛起伏。一个潜泳者
被送回岸边，哦，我见过他
那个小个子爱尔兰人。他说他环绕过
半个地球，有时泅水而行，有时搭乘白帆
还有一次，他骑坐巨鲸穿过了英吉利海峡
对此我深信不疑。作为交换，我也把
我的故事分享给他：在边界出现之前，
我曾负载过一个人类，那时尚无极境
一次漫长的环游过后，我们回到了原点
奇异的是，他拥有了我的双鳍而我
则代他在陆地生活

叙述至此，我们的故事产生了部分交错
关于那片海峡，和它湛蓝色的幽光
如同一道屏障的裂隙，穿过后
又复归平静。遗憾的是
我们并不知道，边界早已显现
并蔓延到了海上

Riding Whales

The bars of the sea rise and fall with the waves. A diver
is brought back to shore – oh, I have seen him,
that little Irishman. He claimed to have circled
half the globe, sometimes swimming, sometimes riding
white sails,
and once, he rode a giant whale through the English
Channel.
I believed him without hesitation. In exchange, I shared
my story with him: before the boundaries appeared,
I once carried a human, back when there were no limits.
After a long journey, we returned to where we'd started.
Strangely, he acquired my fins while I evolved
to live on land for him.

At this point in our narrative, our stories partly overlapped
around that strait and its deep azure light,
like a crack in a barrier, passing through
and returning to calm. Unfortunately,
we didn't know the border had already formed
and spread into the sea.

（彼得·休斯、安文婧 译）

Branches and Leaves
枝 叶

江汀 1986 年生，安徽望江人，现居北京，任职于《十月》杂志，著有诗集《来自邻人的光》《北京和灰尘》，散文集《二十个站台》。

江汀
Jiang Ting

Jiang Ting (b.1986) was born in Wangjiang, Anhui Province. He currently resides in Beijing and works for *October* magazine. His published works include poetry collections such as *Light from My Neighbor* and *Beijing & Dust*, as well as an essay collection *Twenty Platforms*.

枝 叶

枝叶确实漫过了我的身体，
再往上，接触着永远柔和的空气。
我梦见了你，在片刻之内，
在坚硬的、石头累积的旅程里。

我的生命中，既然充满了石头，
当然也布满了这些树影。
正午的阳光下，我似乎继续漫游，
前行又徘徊在这条家园的小径。

越来越苍翠，枝繁叶茂，
再没有别人能理解这种睡意。
可是无法醒来，又无从触摸，
只能倾听着，仿佛它是宿命。

我只能把自己的焦灼献给你，
从始至终，此起彼伏。
每一分，每一秒，我们清清楚楚，
而绿色的颂扬声将超过全部。

Branches and Leaves

Branches and leaves are covering my body,
They touch the constant softness of the air.

I briefly dreamt of you, it was a journey
Amidst hardness, accumulations of stones.

My life is filled with stones,
And a host of tree shadows.

In the midday sunlight, I seem to wander forever,
Moving forwards yet lingering on this homewards path.

Greener and greener, flourishing branches and leaves,
No one else can understand this drowsiness.
Unable to wake up, unable to embrace it,
I can only listen, as if it were destiny.

I dedicate my anxiety to you alone,
From start to finish all along the way.
Every minute, every second, we are clear,
The song of greenness will overwhelm the world.

（彼得·休斯、安文婧 译）

Snow
雪

李啸洋　笔名从安，1986 年生，山西右玉人，现任教于北京电影学院。出版著作《时间赋格：中国电影中的劳动记忆》，诗集《花神的夜晚》。曾获《星星》诗刊年度大学生诗人奖（2017），国家新闻出版广电总局第九届"扶持青年优秀电影剧作计划"奖（2018），全球华语大学生短诗大赛新诗年度诗人奖（2019），第七届扬子江年度青年诗人奖（2022），云时代·新工业诗歌奖·评论奖（2023）等。参加《诗刊》社第 37 届青春诗会，第七届中国诗歌节。

李啸洋
Li Xiaoyang

Li Xiaoyang (b.1986), who writes under the name Cong'an, was born in Youyu, Shanxi Province. He works as a teacher at the Beijing Film Academy. His published works include *Fugue of Time: Labor in the Memory of Chinese Films* and the poetry collection *Night of the Flower Queen*. He received the 2017 Award for Poet of the Year in Universities organized by *Star* Poetry Monthly Magazine, the 2019 Annual Award for New Verse at the Global Competition of Short Chinese Poems by University Students, the 7th Yangtze River Annual Award for Young Poets, and the Commentary Award of the Cloud Era New Industrial Poetry Award in 2023. He participated in the 37th Young Poets' Meeting organized by the *Poetry Periodical* and the 7th China Poetry Festival.

雪

句子尽头，雪开始落下
最后一行雪落在树上，精灵
碎身于泥土中。词语朦胧

起来，乌云穿过无限
竖琴轻轻拨响叹号，画眉的口哨
嘹亮起来。水在天空祈祷
将布道书洒向人间。冰封住
尘世的光芒，地下的
黑陶敞开耳朵
听雪落进时间的瓮中

Snow

At the end of the sentence the snow begins to fall
The last line of snow falls on the trees, wild spirits
broken in the mud. Blurred words

appear, clouds travel through infinity
the harp softly plucks an exclamation mark, the thrush's song
turns louder, water is praying in the sky
delivering sermons to the world. Earthly light
is frozen, ancient black shards underground
open their ears
listen to the snow fall in the urn of time

（彼得·休斯、游心泉 译）

The Girl's Sky
那女孩的星空

杨碧薇　1988 年生于云南昭通，现居北京。诗人、作家、批评家。北京大学艺术学博士后，现任教于鲁迅文学院。出版《下南洋》《去火星旅行》等诗集、散文集、学术批评集共六种。获《十月》诗歌奖、《钟山》之星·青年佳作奖、《诗刊》陈子昂诗歌奖·青年批评家奖、《扬子江诗刊》青年诗人奖·评论奖等。有诗作被译为英、法、日、韩、西、阿等语言。

杨碧薇
Yang Biwei

Yang Biwei (b.1988) was born in Zhaotong, Yunnan Province, and resides in Beijing. She is a poet, writer, and critic. She earned her post-doctoral degree in art from Peking University and teaches at the Lu Xun Literature Academy. Yang has published six books of poetry, essays, and scholarly criticism including *Journey to the South Seas* and *Traveling to Mars*. She has been honored with awards such as the *October* Poetry Award, the Star of *Zhongshan* magazine "Excellent Work of Young Writers", the Chen Zi'ang Poetry Award for Young Critics, and the Young Critic Award of *Yangtze River Poetry* magazine. Some of her poems have been translated into English, French, Japanese, Korean, Spanish, Arabic, etc.

那女孩的星空

整个夜晚，我们在萨热拉村的旷野中看星星：
报幕的是金星，
为它做烤馕的是木星；
很快，银河挥洒开晶钻腰带，
北斗七星舀着新挤的阿富汗牛奶；
猎户和双鱼躲起了猫猫，
天琴座拨响巴朗孜库木。
另一个半球的南十字星耳朵尖，也听得痒痒的，
只好在赤道那头呼唤知音。
十岁的阿拉说："今晚我好开心。
等我长大了，能不能当个宇航员？"
——她瞳孔的荧屏上，一颗滑音般的流星
正穿过天空的琴弦。所有浑浊的事物
都在冷蓝的呼吸里沉淀。
后来，塔吉克人跳累了鹰舞，按亮小屋的彩灯。
魔幻世界倏然隐去，
而某种奇光，已在万星流萤时照进我们心底。

The Girl's Sky

All night we watched the stars over the Sarela Village wilderness:

Venus opened the proceedings,

Jupiter baked flatbread in celebration;

Soon the Milky Way unveiled its crystalline belt,

The Big Dipper ladled fresh Afghan milk;

Orion and Pisces were playing hide-and-seek,

Lyra plucked her resonant strings.

In the other hemisphere, the ears of the Southern Cross tingled,

Compelled to seek a kindred spirit beyond the equator.

Ten-year-old Ala beamed, 'Tonight I feel so happy.

When I grow up, can I become an astronaut?'

—On her pupils' screen, a racing meteor

Flicked across the chords of the sky. All that was murky

Resolved into cool, blue breath.

Later the Tajiks, weary from the Eagle Dance, turned on the
    lights of their huts.

Abruptly, the magical realm receded,

Yet some strange luminescence had entered our hearts

amidst the countless stars.

（彼得·休斯、安文婧 译）

295

Vagary of Smoke
烟　枝

肖水　男，1980年生于湖南郴州，诗人、作家、译者，复旦大学文学博士。现执教于上海大学文学院中国创意写作研究院。出版有诗集《失物认领》《中文课》《艾草：新绝句诗集》《渤海故事集：小说诗诗集》《两日晴，郁达夫：绝句小说诗》，以及《渤海故事集》（中英对照）、《肖水诗选》（俄文），合译《草坪的复仇》《布劳提根诗选》《在美国钓鳟鱼》。曾获未名诗歌奖、《上海文学》诗歌新人奖、诗探索奖·新锐奖、三月三诗会奖、第二届建安文学奖、《诗刊》2023年度陈子昂诗歌奖·青年诗人奖。

肖水
Xiao Shui

Xiao Shui (b.1980) was born in Chenzhou, Hu'nan Province, is a poet, writer, and translator. He received his PhD degree in literature from Fudan University. He teaches creative writing at Liberal Arts College in Shanghai University. His published works include poetry collections *Lost and Found*, *Chinese Lessons*, *Mugwort: A Collection of New Quatrains*, *Bohai Stories*: *A Collection of Novel Poems*, *Two Sunny Days*, *Yu Dafu*: *Novel Poems in Quatrain*, as well as a Chinese-English bilingual edition of *Bohai Stories* and a selection of his poems translated into Russian. He has co-translated Richard Brautigan's *Revenge of the Lawn*, *The Pill Versus the Springhill Mine Disaster*, and *Trout Fishing in America*. Xiao Shui has won the Weiming Poetry Award, the *Shanghai Literature* magazine Poetry Award for Newcomer, *Poetry Exploration's* Emerging Poet Award, the March 3rd Poetry Festival Award, the 2nd Jian'an Literature Award, and the 2023 Chen Zi'ang Young Poet of the Year Award.

烟 枝

他比我先下飞机。冬日凛冽的天气里，所有能看见的
几乎都是新的。出租车终于在二马路滨海广场前面停
　了下来，
将要路演的老年剧团，正从皮卡上，往外搬运琵琶和
　二胡。
酒店房间恰可俯视他们，他们小小的，脸上的油彩不
　带任何折痕。

Vagary of Smoke

He got off the plane before me. In the cold winter, everything in sight

was almost new. The taxi finally stopped near the Second Street of Marina Square,

The old troupe, setting up a roadshow, was unloading the lutes and erhus out of the pickup.

Looking down from the hotel room, their small, oily faces had no creases.

（Noelle Noell 译）

Sitting Alone in the Rain
雨中独坐

余退 1983 年出生，浙江温州人，中国作家协会会员，温州大学创意写作研究中心特邀作家，入选浙江省"新荷计划"人才库，出版诗集《春天符》《夜晚潜泳者》及短篇小说集《贝壳剧院》。

余退
Yu Tui

Yu Tui (b.1983) was born in Wenzhou, Zhejiang Province and is a member of the China Writers Association. Yu serves as a guest writer at the Creative Writing Research Center of Wenzhou University and has been selected as a member of the talent pool of Zhejiang Province's "New Lotus Plan". He has published the poetry collections *Spring Talisman* and *Night Swimmer,* as well as the short story collection *The Shell Theater.*

雨中独坐

在更暴虐的雨来临之前，我坐在
我家阳台爬升的绿植之间
晚春还是带来了疗愈的功效
倔强的小男孩又回来了，有几次
幼稚的我激励中年的我：
生命是沉浸。我们一起坐在铁艺椅上
我像将儿子抱在腿上玩耍的父亲
激荡着双重的勇气和喜悦
仰视着空中的雨浇着
头顶的藤叶，雨滴纷纷跳动着
顺着叶子滑落到另一片叶子上
我的头发已经湿了，接着是
我的脖子，我的惭愧，我的尾脊

Sitting Alone in the Rain

Before the more violent rain arrived, I sat
Among the green climbing plants on my balcony.
Late spring still brings its healing effects.
The stubborn little boy returned and several times,
The childish self inspired the middle-aged self.
Life is immersion. We sat together on the iron chair,
I was like a father playing with his son on his lap,
Stirring up double the courage and joy,
Looking up at the sky as the rain poured
Onto the vine leaves above. The raindrops dance,
Sliding from one leaf to another.
My hair was wet, and then
My neck, my shame, my backside.

（彼得·休斯、安文婧 译）

Village School
村 小

张二棍 本名张常春，1982 年生于山西代县，武汉文学院签约专业作家。出版有诗集《搬山寄》《入林记》等。曾获《诗刊》年度青年诗人奖、华文青年诗人奖、李杜青年诗人奖、《诗歌周刊》年度诗人等。

张二棍
Zhang Ergun

Zhang Ergun (b.1982) was born in Daixian, Shanxi Province. He is a professional writer under contract to the Wuhan College of Chinese Literature. He has published poetry collections such as *Moving Mountains* and *Into the Woods*. He has been singled out as the Young Poet of the Year by the *Poetry Periodical* and the Poet of the Year by *Poetry Weekly*. He is also winner of the Chinese Young Poets Award, and the Li Bai & Du Fu Young Poet Award.

村 小

1
我来迟了，满怀愧疚坐下来
——尘埃四起的教室，摇摇欲坠的课桌
我是这无垠时空中，懵懂的小学生
听腊月西风，这位无色无相的
大先生，携带着宇宙深处的教诲
从无垠中赶来，为我传授
一堂，凛冽的自然课

2
我捡起，遗落墙角的一粒
粉笔，在斑驳的黑板上
写着，画着。于这刺骨的
寒风中，画出怒放于另一座
大陆的奇花。于这无人的僻壤上
写下，一枚枚震古烁今的名字
——我要独自赓续，那业已中断的教育
我要躬身肃立，教化那个冥顽的自己

3
一面墙，和半个屋顶
都塌了。麻雀们无忧穿行，自在嬉闹
偶尔，在梁柱间小憩，滴溜溜
转动着小脑袋，仿佛一群
三心二意的旁听生，被留在这里
自习。它们叽叽喳喳，翻来覆去
仿佛争辩着，一个永远
回答不上来的问题

Village School

1

I was late, and guiltily sat down,
In the dusty classroom, with wobbly desks.
I'm an ignorant school kid in this endless space and time,
Listening to the west wind in December, this colorless, formless
Teacher, bringing learning from the depths of the universe,
Emerging from infinity to bring me
A chilling lesson about nature.

2

I picked up chalk from a dusty corner and I wrote and drew
On the mottled blackboard. In this biting cold wind I sketched
Exotic flowers from another continent. In this desolate land
I wrote down startling and unexpected names.
I want to continue my interrupted education alone,
I want to stand tall, and teach the stubborn self.

3

One wall and half the roof have collapsed.
The sparrows fly around without a care,
Sometimes perching on the beams, turning their heads
Like a group of bored, forgotten clerks.
They chirp and argue, as if discussing
A question that can never be resolved.

（彼得·休斯、安文婧 译）

Cherry
樱 桃

张小末　本名陈超，浙江省作协会员，浙江省新荷人才，杭州市青年文艺人才，著有个人诗集《致某某》《生活的修辞学》，作品散见《诗刊》《北京文学》《江南诗》《山西文学》等刊物。

张小末
Zhang Xiaomo

Zhang Xiaomo is a member of the Zhejiang Provincial Writers Association, member of the talent pool of Zhejiang Province's "New Lotus Plan" and a young literary talent in Hangzhou city. She has authored poetry collections *To Someone* and *The Rhetoric of Life*. Her works have been published in various magazines such as the *Poetry Periodical*, *Beijing Literature*, *Jiangnan Poetry*, and *Shanxi Literature*.

樱 桃

七岁。她小小的身子
微红的脸,鞋子沾着一点泥
她的旧棉袄
袖子口露出了棉絮,雪一样白

十九岁。她提着两袋行李
羞涩地站在大学门口
寝室里的女孩们谈论明星和流行品牌
她在公共浴室无所适从,犹豫着
打了水回到宿舍

二十八岁。她给刚出生的孩子哺乳
盘子里放着樱桃
这酸酸的,来不及熟透的果实。那么小
像多年前
她曾在浴室紧紧捂着的身体

Cherry

Seven years old. Her small body
Reddish face, mud-stained shoes,
Her old cotton jacket,
The padding exposed at the cuffs, as white as snow.

At nineteen she carries two cases,
Stands shyly at the university gate.
The dormitory girls discuss celebrities, designer brands,
She feels lost in the shared bathrooms, hesitates,
Gets water and returns to her dorm.

At twenty-eight she breastfeeds her new baby,
A plate of cherries sits nearby.
Sour, unripened fruit. So small
Like the body she kept hidden
In the bathroom all those years ago.

（彼得・休斯、安文婧 译）

Xi Meng
希 孟

赵汗青　1997 年生，山东烟台人，毕业于北京大学中文系。从事戏剧创作，代表作话剧《桃花扇 1912》。出版有诗集《红楼里的波西米亚》。曾获光华诗歌奖，参加《诗刊》社第 38 届青春诗会，第 12 届十月诗会等。

青春，如风有信

赵汗青
Zhao Hanqing

Zhao Hanqing (b.1997) was born in Yantai, Shandong Province. She graduated from the Department of Chinese Language and Literature of Peking University. Zhao has written many plays, most notably *Peach Blossom Fan 1912*. She has also published a poetry collection *Bohemia in the Red Chamber*. She won the Guanghua Poetry Award and participated in the 38th Young Poets' Meeting organized by the *Poetry Periodical* and *October* magazine's 12th Poetry Conference.

希 孟

那个字迹秀美的宰相
创造了我。九百年前，他的字
如风吹马群，奔袭起
我散乱的命运。十八岁就
做天才的人是这样
二十岁就死的人
是这样。六行字。它狭窄到，都不够形容
我在人生最后一次生日宴上
看过的星星。当然了
我当然知道，很多人活出了我
几倍的寿命，却依然没有丞相
为他留名。这有什么办法呢？
在照亮宇宙和照亮冰河之间，我选择了
照亮纸

我选择了成为砚台上的
孙悟空，绢纸上的小哪吒
用婉转的手翻起
雨的风火轮。他们在楼上、
在舟中听雨。我在汴梁的
耳蜗里听雨，在雨的身体里听雨

Xi Meng

The prime minister with elegant handwriting
Created me. Nine hundred years ago, his writing
Was like wind through a herd of horses,
Arranging the seeds of my fate.
This is how it is with those
Who become geniuses at eighteen
And are dead by the age of twenty.
Six lines of words don't seem enough to describe
The stars I saw at my very last birthday party.
I know many have lived for far longer than I could
But no prime minister has preserved their names.
That is simply how things are.
Illuminate the universe or illuminate the glacier?
I choose to illuminate the paper.
I chose to become the Monkey King on the ink stone,
Little Nezha on the silk paper, turning the wind
And fire wheels in the rain with graceful agility.
They listen to the rain upstairs, or in the boat.
I listen to the rain in my head in Bianliang,
And I listened to the rain within the moving sky.

天给我颜色，天给我雨……雨
我相信雨曾平等地淋湿过我
和他，淋湿他可能苦吟过的
宋元明清。雨滋润出的青草
织起我们，古董商的巧手
抚平我们——我就这样窃走了
他金碧恢弘的一生
用我的名字——它孤零零地掉落在
一个马上就要破灭的王朝里，像两颗
空洞的回声掉入
一个白昼的雨

十八岁的是我不是你。我懒散
贪玩，每天在画中的亭台里
叼着酒壶闲晃。我想斗鸡走犬，想一事无成
想嚼着没有辣味的炊饼然后
变成天上不加盐的云。而你
你是冬夜里枯坐的人
雪是灯油，眼泪是灯油
点滴着，就坐成了一尊
山的守夜人。抽筋的手指
会在梦中，颤抖出一道新的河

The heavens gave me color, the heavens gave me rain… rain.

I believe the rain has fallen equally on him and myself,

And soaked the lines he might have recited throughout

The ancient Dynasties of Song, Yuan, Ming and Qing.

The green grass nourished by the rain has woven us,

We have been burnished by the deft hands of antiquarians.

I have stolen his magnificent life with my name –

A name that falls through a failing dynasty

Empty echoes falling through the daytime rain.

Now I'm the one who is eighteen, not you. I am lazy,

Playful, wandering daily through the painted pavilions

With a wine glass in my hand. I want frivolous pursuits

Such as cockfights and dog racing, I want to do nothing,

But swallow bland pancakes and then turn into

Featureless clouds in the sky. But you,

You are the one who sits through the cold winter nights,

With snow and tears as your lamp oil. Dripping,

You sit like the mountain's nightwatchman.

Cramped fingers will tremble in your dreams

To create a brand-new river.

我是你茫茫真迹的一生中

最大的赝品——蓝是真迹

绿是真迹; 山是真迹

剥落是真迹。我们会在蒙住眼睛的

地府里相遇, 像两只

断掉的左手和断掉的右手

别扭地紧握。来, 让我们在大宋灭亡之后

再共同创造一种美。我去看

你去呼吸。我们

"分明是一位美少年。他只能十八岁

他不可能老。"

也不可能长高。我们是

拟人的颜色, 是颜色都

灰飞烟灭的舞蹈

——致舞者张翰

注: 有一说为《千里江山图》乃清初收藏家梁清标集蔡京跋（1114 年）、李溥光跋（1303 年）与无名氏巨幅青绿山水画拼贴"再创作"的艺术品, 并杜撰出了一个"王希孟"天才早逝的故事。（见曹星原:《王之希孟——〈千里江山图〉的国宝之路》）

I am the biggest fake among all the true works

Of your lifetime: blue is authentic, so is green;

The mountain is authentic, as are the signs of ageing.

We will meet in the blindfolded underworld

Like two severed hands, awkwardly clasped.

Come, together let's create a new beauty

After the fall of the Song Dynasty. I will watch,

You will breathe. We 'Clearly are a beautiful young man.

Forever eighteen, he cannot grow old.' Nor will he grow taller.

We are personified colors. We are a dance

Where all the colors vanish into ashes.

—To the dancer Zhang Han

Note: Some believe the artwork "A Thousand Miles of Rivers and Mountains"
is a re-creation by collector Liang Qingbiao in the early Qing Dynasty, placing
inscriptions by Cai Jing (1114) and Li Puguang (1303) on an anonymous large
blue-green landscape painting, based on which he fabricated the story of the
prodigy Wang Ximeng who died young. (See Cao Xingyuan: *Wang Ximeng and
the National Treasure A Thousand Miles of Rivers and Mountains*).

（彼得·休斯、黄心怡 译）

The Shaper for Xiaotiaotiao
赋形者——致小跳跳

胡桑　1981 年生于浙江德清。诗人、译者。同济大学哲学博士、德国波恩大学访问学者、中国现代文学馆特邀研究员，现为同济大学中文系副教授。著有诗集《赋形者》《你我面目》《比海更多的海》。散文集《在孟溪那边》。评论集《隔渊望着人们》《始于一次分神》。译有《我曾这样寂寞生活：辛波斯卡诗选》《染匠之手：奥登随笔集》《生活研究：洛威尔诗选》《旧金山海湾幻景：米沃什随笔集》等。曾获未名诗歌奖、柔刚诗歌奖等。

胡桑
Hu Sang

Hu Sang (b.1981), poet and translator, was born in Deqing, Zhejiang Province. He received his PhD from Tongji University and was a visiting scholar to the University of Bonn, Germany. He is an associate professor in the Department of Chinese Language and Literature at Tongji University. He is the author of poetry collections such as *The Shaper*, *The Face of You and Me* and *More Seas Beyond the Sea*. He has also published prose collection *Over the River Mengxi* and two collections of commentaries *Looking at People Across the Abyss* and *Beginning with a Distraction*. He has translated *I Have Lived Such a Lonely Life*: *Selected Poems of Wisława Szymborska*, *The Dyer's Hand* (by W. H. Auden), *Life Studies*: *Selected Poems of Robert Lowell*, and *Vision of San Francisco Bay* (by Czesław Miłosz). He has won the Weiming Poetry Award and the Rougang Poetry Award, among others.

赋形者

——致小跳跳

尝试过各种可能性之后，
你退入一个小镇。雨下得正是时候，
把事物收拢进轻盈的水雾。

度日是一门透明的艺术。你变得
如此谦逊，犹如戚浦塘，在光阴中
凝聚，学习如何检测黄昏的深度。

你出入生活，一切不可解释，从果园，
散步到牙医诊所，再驱车，停在小学门口，
几何学无法解析这条路线，它随时溢出。

鞋跟上不规则的梦境，也许有毒，
那些忧伤比泥土还要密集，但是你醒在
一个清晨，专心穿一只鞋子，

生活，犹如麦穗鱼，被你收服在
漆黑的内部。日复一日，你制造轻易的形式，
抵抗混乱，使生活有了寂静的形状。

我送来的秋天，被你种植在卧室里，
"返回内部才是救赎。"犹如柿子，
体内的变形使它走向另一种成熟。

The Shaper
for Xiaotiaotiao

Having tried a number of possibilities,
You withdraw into a small town. It's raining at the right time;
The rain gathers everything into light fog.

Living your life is a transparent art. You become as humble
As the Qipu River you live beside. You hold yourself back
In time, and learn to measure the depth of dusk.

You enter and exit life; most things cannot be explained.
You wander from orchard to dentist, then drive
To the gate of the schoolyard, a route
Unknown through geometry; it can overflow at any moment.

Irregular dreams on the heel might be toxic;
Sorrow is denser than clay, but you wake
In the morning, focused on wearing a shoe.

Like a flowerhorn fish, your life is tamed
For a dark interior. Day by day, to counteract disorder,
And shape life into silence, you make an easy form.

Autumn has been planted in the bedroom.
'Returning inward is redemption.' Your body is transformed
Like a persimmon, and autumn has another kind of ripeness.

（胡桑、Brenda Hillman 译）

Night Road
夜　路

談骁　1987 年生于湖北恩施。现为长江文艺出版社诗歌中心主编，湖北省文学院签约专业作家，出版诗集《以你之名》《涌向平静》《说时迟》。曾获《长江文艺》诗歌双年奖、华文青年诗人奖、扬子江青年诗人奖。

谈骁
Tan Xiao

Tan Xiao (b.1987) was born in Enshi, Hubei Province, and is the chief editor of the Poetry Center at Yangtze River Literature and Art Publishing House and a professional writer under the contract to the Hubei Provincial Academy of Literature. He has published poetry collections *In Your Name*, *Surging Towards Calmness*, and *Speaking of Lateness*. He has been honored with several awards, including the *Yangtze River Literature and Art* Biennial Poetry Award, the Chinese Young Poets Award, and the Yangtze River Annual Award for Young Poets.

夜 路

父亲把杉树皮归成一束，
那是最好的火把。他举着点燃的树皮
走在黑暗中，每当火焰旺盛，
他就捏紧树皮，让火光暗下来，
似乎漆黑的长路不需要过于明亮的照耀。
一路上，父亲都在控制燃烧的幅度，
他要用手中的树皮领我们走完夜路。
一路上，我们说了不少话，
声音很轻，脚步声也很轻，
像几团面目模糊的影子。
而火把始终可以自明，
当它暗淡，火星仍在死灰中闪烁；
当它持久地明亮，那是快到家了。
父亲抖动手腕，夜风吹走死灰，
再也不用俭省，再也不用把夜路
当末路一样走，火光蓬勃，
把最后的路照得明亮无比，
我们也通体亮堂，像从巨大的光明中走出。

Night Road

Father would bundle pine bark into a torch,

a proper torch. He held the lit bark,

and walked through the darkness. Whenever the flame flared up,

he would squeeze the bark to dim the light,

as if the pitch-black road didn't need too much illumination.

Throughout the journey, Father controlled the burning,

guiding us with the bark in his hand along the night road.

We talked a lot along the way,

with soft voices, light footsteps,

like indistinct shadows.

The torch always illuminated itself,

even when it dimmed, sparks flickered in the ashes;

when it burned steadily bright, we knew we were close to
home.

Father shook his wrist, and the night wind blew away the
ashes.

There was no need to be frugal anymore, no need to treat
the night road

as if it were the end; the fire flared up vigorously,

illuminating brightly the last stretch of road,

and we were illuminated too, as if emerging from a great
light.

（彼得·休斯、安文婧 译）

Wings Above the Mortal World
高出人世的翅膀

桑 子　浙江省作协第十届全委会委员，绍兴市作协副主席。著有《栖真之地》《德克萨斯》《柠檬树》《雨中静止的火车》《野性的时间》《向天空拉满弓》等诗集、长篇小说和散文集十余部，曾获浙江省优秀文学作品奖、扬子江诗学奖、滇池文学奖、李白诗歌奖、紫金·江苏文学期刊优秀作品奖等。

桑 子
Sang Zi

Sang Zi, a member of the 10th Committee of the Zhejiang Provincial Writers Association and the Vice President of the Shaoxing Municipal Writers Association, has published over ten collections of poetry, novels, and essays, including *A Place the Truth Resides in*, *Texas*, *Lemon Tree*, *The Train That Stopped in the Rain*, *Wild Time*, and *Drawing a Bow Towards the Sky*. Sang Zi has been honored with awards including the Award for Outstanding Literary Works in Zhejiang, the Yangtze River Poetry Award, the Dianchi Literary Award, the Li Bai Poetry Award, and the Zijin-Jiangsu Literary Journal Award for Outstanding Works.

高出人世的翅膀

山是人的另一副骨架

现在太阳布下浓荫

与黑夜别无二致

灵鹫教会所有眼睛可怕的平衡术

关于未来的狂想

比果实的内核更准确

深入所有人强烈的渴望中

寺庙在一条溪流的尽头

有些地方不需要抵达

无限就在此

在一张旧照片看到果实成熟

死亡多沉重

造山运动以反向的力让它变轻

无可抵达的尽头

有翅膀高出人世

松针上行走的人

陷入光的沙丘，无计脱身

植物庞大的根系藏着巨大的激情

过去它们是大海和流云

现在是一个人的身体和灵魂

Wings Above the Mortal World

The mountain is mankind's other skeleton.

The sun casts dense shadows

Similar to night.

The eagle teaches all eyes the terrible art of balance.

Wild thoughts about the future,

More detailed than the core of fruit

Deep within the people's fierce desires.

The temple stands by the end of a stream,

Some places do not need to be reached,

Infinity is here.

In an old photograph the fruit is ripening,

The vast weight of death, lightened by the forces

raising mountains up into the light,

an end that can never be reached.

Wings glide above the world.

People tread on beds of pine needles,

or sink in dunes of light with no escape.

The huge root systems of plants conceal great passion.

In the past they were the sea and clouds,

Now they are the body – they are the soul.

（彼得·休斯、安文婧 译）

Now
现 在

梁书正 1985年生，湖南湘西人，苗族。湖南省诗歌学会常务理事，湘西州作协副主席。出版诗集《遍地繁花》《群山祈祷》《唯有悲伤无人认领》等。曾获紫金人民文学之星诗歌奖，红高粱诗歌奖，沈从文文学奖等奖项。入选湖南省文艺人才"三百工程"。曾参加《诗刊》社第38届青春诗会，《人民文学》"新浪潮"诗会，湖南省第七届青创会，全国少数民族文学创作会议。

青春，如风有信

梁书正
Liang Shuzheng

Liang Shuzheng (b.1985) was born in Xiangxi, Hu'nan Province, and is of Miao ethnicity. He is the standing director of the Board of the Hu'nan Provincial Poetry Society and the Vice President of the Xiangxi Prefecture Writers Association. He has published poetry collections *Flowers Everywhere*, *Prayer of the Mountains*, and *Unclaimed Sadness*. Liang Shuzheng has received accolades including the Zijin-*People's Literature* Poetry Award, the Red Sorghum Poetry Award, and the Shen Congwen Literature Award. Additionally, he participated in the 38th Young Poets' Meeting held by the *Poetry Periodical*, the "New Wave" Poetry Meeting held by *People's Literature*, the 7th Hu'nan Provincial Conference for Young Writers' Literary Creation, and the National Literature Conference for Ethnic Minorities.

现 在

现在，这里种满南瓜、豌豆、白菜和香葱
这里绿油油的，还开着小花儿

现在，我的喜悦是方形的，成块，成片
它落在每一颗蔬菜上

现在，我是个小农民，我有锄头和种子
还有枝头上欢叫的喜鹊儿

现在，谁爱上我，就和我种地
谁愿嫁我，就和我卖菜

Now

Now pumpkins, peas, cabbages and chives grow here
It's lush and full of little flowers.

Now my joy is set out in squares, in patches,
It falls on every crop.

Now I am a small farmer, I have a hoe and seeds,
And magpies call cheerfully from the branches.

Now whoever falls in love with me will farm with me,
Whoever marries me, we will market the vegetables together.

（彼得·休斯、安文婧 译）

Dreams are Like Long Journeys
入梦宛如一次远行

熊焱 1980 年生，贵州瓮安人，现居成都。《草堂》执行主编。著有诗集 4 本、长篇小说 2 部。曾获华文青年诗人奖、茅盾新人奖、艾青诗歌奖、陈子昂诗歌奖等各种奖项。

熊焱
Xiong Yan

Xiong Yan (b.1980) was born in Weng'an, Guizhou Province, and lives in Chengdu. He is the executive editor-in-chief of the poetry magazine *Thatched Cottage* and has published four poetry collections and two novels. Xiong Yan has been the recipient of many awards, including the Chinese Young Poets Award, Mao Dun Literary Award for Young Writers, Ai Qing Poetry Award, and the Chen Zi'ang Poetry Award.

入梦宛如一次远行

每次从梦里醒来，都是从另一个时空中

回到了现实。有时我走得太远太急

归来时满身疲倦。有时我历经刺激的冒险

获得了意外的愉悦。有时我遭遇悲惨的变故

我哭疼了全世界的伤心……

当记忆在时间的弯曲中变得恍惚

我会忘记梦境。当记忆沿着时间的顺时针向前

我会想起梦境，仿佛人生只在眨眼的瞬息

如果我梦见了往事，那是我穿越时间

回到了过去。如果我梦见了陌生的场景

那是我在探寻时间无尽的边界

哦，生命是一场悲欢离合的苦役

命运从不怜悯这人生马不停蹄的艰辛

每次我从梦里醒来，都是从另一个时空中

回到了现实。山河有序，群星运行

我带着白发与皱纹，岁月带着沉默与生死

Dreams are Like Long Journeys

Every time I wake from dreams I return to reality as if

From another time and place. Sometimes I've gone too far, too fast

And I'm exhausted. Sometimes I've had thrilling adventures

And harvested unexpected joy. Sometimes I've encountered
  tragic misfortunes

And wept for the sorrows of the world...

When memories blur in time's distortions

I may forget my dreams. When memories move to the rhythms of
  the clock

I may remember my dreams as if life passed by in the blink of an eye.

If I dream of the past, then I travel through time returning

To years gone by. If I dream of unfamiliar scenes

Then I'm exploring the endless boundaries of time.

Oh, life is a bitter cycle of joys and then sorrows,

Fate never pities the endless hardships of our lives.

Every time I wake from dreams I return to reality as if

From another time and place. The mountains and rivers

are as they were and the stars move on their courses.

I have grey hair and wrinkles, and the years bring

silence, life, then death.

（彼得·休斯、黄心怡 译）

Snow Falling in Qianmen
雪落在前门

戴潍娜 1985 年生于江苏南通，诗人、学者。毕业于牛津大学，现为中国社会科学院外国文学研究所副研究员，出版诗集《灵魂体操》《以万物为情人》《我的降落伞坏了》等，戏剧《侵犯》《水泥玫瑰》，翻译有《天鹅绒监狱》等。主编翻译诗刊《光年》。曾获 2017 太平洋国际诗歌奖年度诗人，2020 剑桥徐志摩银柳叶青年诗歌奖。

戴潍娜
Dai Weina

Dai Weina (b.1985), a poet and scholar, was born in Nantong, Jiangsu Province. She graduated from the University of Oxford and is an associate researcher at the Institute of Foreign Literature in Chinese Academy of Social Sciences. Dai Weina has published several poetry collections, including *Soul Exercises*, *Loving All Things*, and *My Parachute is Broken*, as well as plays such as *Invasion* and *Concrete Roses*. She is the translator of Miklós Haraszti's *L'artiste d'Etat* and the editor-in-chief of *Light Years*, a review of translated foreign poems. She was honored as Poet of the Year at the 2017 Pacific International Poetry Festival and the Silver Willow Award for Young Poets in 2020 Cambridge Xu Zhimo Festival.

雪落在前门

究竟 是哪一年的牌楼, 哪一年的雪
牵引这幻变的中轴线

蹬上老字号靴子
鹅毛天赴约
眼前每一条路都失去了分别
若仅仅害怕滑倒,
我并不介意光脚 凌云健步

大雪, 从中国的最北方一路赶来
走到今天 不改洁白

飘在鲜鱼口的糖葫芦上,
就是甜的冰衣;
落在黑天里,
便与乌贼对读
旧时旧梦 如宵鸣的白鸟
飞出严实的人间

邀请这个世界完完整整下一场雪
——许多年来我以为自己不配
碎落的星空 毫不妥协
幸好认出 它们就是那年消失的雪人
分明已是三月, 谢谢雪
为我再下了一次

Snow Falling in Qianmen

Which year's archway, which year's snow
Guides this shifting central axis?

I put on these old-fashioned boots
For my appointment with the goose-feathered sky.
Every path in front of me has lost its definition.
If it weren't for the fear of slipping,
I would be happy to walk barefoot.

The heavy snow has come from the far north of China
It is unchanged in its whiteness.

Settling on the candied hawthorn at Xianyukou,
It becomes a sweet coating of ice;
Falling through the darkening skies
It reads like an ancient story
Old dreams resemble white birds singing at night
Flying away from the world of common sense.

I invite this world to snow utterly –
For many years I thought I was unworthy.
The shattered starry sky does not relent.
I realise with joy that these are the snowmen
   who disappeared that year.
Though it is already March, I thank the snow
for falling once again for me.

（彼得·休斯、安文婧 译）

A Grand Gathering of Civilization

文明的盛会

生命的体认，爱与希望的色彩
Experience of life, Colors of love and hope

国际
青春诗会
International Youth Poetry Festival

First International Youth Poetry Festival Special Session for BRICS Countries

جوان
Молодость
青春 Youth
الشباب जवानी
Juventude

Long Distance
Separates
No Bosom Friends

天涯若比邻

Poetry and Thought: Academic Dialogue and Resonance due to Youth

Youth is accompanied by poetry, and the world is sharing at this moment. On the afternoon of July 20th, the academic dialogue of "The First International Youth Poetry Festival - Special Session for BRICS Countries" was held as scheduled. 20 poets from the ten BRICS countries gathered together to focus on the theme of "Innovation of Poetry" and deeply discussed the core topics of poetry such as its role, function, prospect and the possibility and necessity of innovation of poetry in today's world.

Shi Zhanjun, a member of the Party Leadership Group of the China Writers Association, Secretary of the Secretariat, and the Editor-in-Chief of *People's Literature*, gave a speech first. "Perhaps, it is youth that is looking for poetry, and the look of poetry is the look of youth; meanwhile, poetry also illuminates youth, and the people who love poetry are always young." It is the natural role of poetry in facilitating communication and increasing exchanges, bringing together people from different regions and with different beliefs, embracing the pluralistic national cultures, bridging differences, enriching the world's colorfulness, and achieving "harmony in diversity". Shi Zhanjun hopes that everyone will widen their horizons and visions, form ties of friendship, and jointly contribute to promoting the prosperity and development of the poetry of the world.

Li Shaojun, the Editor-in-Chief of the *Poetry Periodical*, and poet Zhao Si hosted the forum's four sessions of dialogue.

Poetry mends the soul and explores the poetic meaning of all things

Five female poets start the dialogue around the theme of "Experience of Life, Colors of Love and Hope". In their view, poetry is not only an art of language, but also a soothing of the soul. With its primitive and powerful strength, poetry challenges the impetuousness of the digital age, connects the common experiences and emotions of mankind, mends people's hearts, and conveys the message of love and peace.

Brazilian poet Ana Rüsche believes that poetry, as a primitive form of human language, has the power to challenge the fast-moving consumer culture in the modern digital age. Poetry can give meaning to seemingly meaningless things and express the deep emotional experience of human beings. Poetry innovation in the 21st century needs to face the challenge of technological progress and use technology to achieve its own development. Russian poet Evgeniia Uliankina believes that poetry itself is an exploration of new things. She compares a poem to "a leap into the unknown" and a "wormhole" connecting different points in time and space. The innovation of poetry is not in experimentation or finding new ways of expression, but in whether poetry can lead readers to new places and bring them changes and surprises. Egyptian poet Nagat Ali regards poetry as an adventurous and innovative journey to explore the poetic meanings of all things. Poets should fight against the traditional beliefs of closed society by "re-evaluating all values". Poetry should express the poet's personal concerns and problems, rather than just serving as a mouthpiece for the collective voice. Saudi Arabian poet Rawan Talal believes that poetry is like a mirror, reflecting the spirit of the times and the details of personal life. Innovation in poetry should not be limited to form, but should cover a wide range of themes and content to adapt to the ever-changing cultural and technological environment, and ultimately make poetry a bridge connecting common human experiences and emotions. UAE poet Shaikha Almteiri mentions that the language of poetry is not limited by geography and language, and is a common language for all mankind. As the master of fantasy and dreams, poets should also draw inspiration from various experiences in life, and through constant self-renewal and exploration, create works that are both personnalité and touching. Only by keeping an open mind and looking for new perspectives and expressions from different cultures and lives can the vitality of poetry be truly stimulated.

Poets seek innovation and change, pursuing the glory of poetry

What is the innovation of poetry? Poetry is like a river, and every poet is an explorer of this river. They use innovative language and form to find new ways to speak to the world. As the poets who discussed about "Eternal is new, writing a poem is to innovate" say, the innovation of poetry lies not only in the exploration of form, but also in its profound connotation and authenticity, and in its confidence in the display of beauty and the victory of goodness.

Brazilian poet Thiago Ponce regards poetry as "the form par excellence of writing ", pointing out that modern poetry always tries to take risks in language and uses writing "to think the new within writing". Poems creation is a new way of breathing. By constantly trying the combination of words, sounds and meanings and new ways of expression, it dialogues with the world in a unique voice and establishes new connections. Each poem is a new discovery and a new recognition of existence and language itself. Russian poet Viacheslav Glazyrin recalls his relationship with Lao Tzu's *Tao Te Ching* and believes that the real "newness" of poetry is not the superficial change, but the inner and eternal "newness" of poetry. He declares that "eternity is new", "reality is new", "facing the unspeakable is new", "elegance and simplicity is new", and "seriousness is new", calling on poets to restore their awe of words and create poems with depth and authenticity to fight against the impetuousness and shallowness of the times. Indian poet Nikhilesh Mishra talks about poetry as a bridge connecting individuals with the greater whole, bringing people closer to spiritual homeland. Despite the rapid development of technology, the core value of poetry as an art form that expresses common human emotions and experiences has not changed. The innovation of poetry is deeply rooted in the sources of human cultures and historical intelligence. Only when poetry is "thrived in hardship and perished in easiness" like human civilizations that evolved in scarcities can it retain its true vitality. By reviewing the development of poetry from ancient times to nowadays, Hassan Alnajjar, a poet from the United Arab Emirates, believes that poetry is as constant as the sky. Its core of expressing human emotions and experiences has not changed. What has changed is the way we look at it. The real innovation of poetry comes from the poet's originality and imagination, which is reflected in the unique way of constructing the structure of poems and the poet's re-imagination and connection of reality. Saudi Arabian poet Hatim Alshehri believes that although novels are a popular literary form, poetry connects people of different cultures, languages and generations in a unique way, enhancing empathy and understanding. Poetry looks at the world from a new perspective, is a profound tool for self-exploration, is an important spiritual therapy, has a role in social struggle, and protects language and aesthetic heritage. "Poetry is the pearl of literature, a dignified elder who never ages..."

Innovation is the main weapon of the god of poetry

"Can the God of Poetry defeat the new gods?" The poets have in-depth exchanges and discussions around this topic. They talked about how poetry connects the past and the future, tradition and modernity, and captures the pulse of the times. The main weapon of the God of Poetry is innovation, which is the pure language and form that penetrates into the human spiritual world.

Egyptian poet Sharif Al-Shafiey believes that digitalization is not only a technological change, but also a new way of experiencing and perceiving life, representing the spirit and philosophy of our time. Digitalization is profoundly changing the composing, circulation and acceptance of poetry. The new growth point of poetry is to deeply exploit the impact of digitalization on human life and explore the intrinsic connection between poetry and digital technology. Poets should embrace the opportunities brought by digitalization. Iranian poet Kianoosh Khan Mohammadi reflects on the two revolutions faced by poetry. One is the emergence of motion pictures. After nearly two centuries, the god of poetry has been able to use animation for its own benefit, and the richness of its expression forms has surpassed animation. The second is the current advance of the artificial intelligence. So far, although artificial intelligence can imitate and even participate in the process of poetry creating to a certain extent, the poetry produced by AI algorithms still lacks real innovation. The main weapon of the god of poetry is innovation, which does not seem to be mastered yet by AI at present. By questioning the inherent concept of what art should be, South African poet Alfred Schaffer talked about art belonging to the public domain, and whether it needs to meet the expectations of romance, politics or other social labels, which made him doubtful. He believes that poetry and art can reveal and criticize the problems of the reality, inspire emotions, shocks and reflections, which is the true value of art. He advocates that poetry avoid mediocrity and self-indulgence, seek novelty, and challenge the audience's expectations. Iranian poet Kazem Vaezzadeh analyzes the importance of "discovery" in poems creating and its subsequent exploration and expansion, advocating that poets should further dig deep and create after the discovery, explore their thinking, expand their imagination, and construct a more organic and phenomenal poetic text world. Chinese poet Hu Sang says that although modern life tends to be transparent and convenient, poems creating must have the courage to explore the deep experience of "reality" rather than simple narration or reproduction of the life itself. In the modern world with plenty of data flowing, poets should explore the deeper level of emotional and meaning mobility, activating the writing world and the poet's subject, and find unique expression and value in the data age.

Mother tongue brings unique value to poetry creation

To insist in writing locally or internationally, individually or collectively? Poetry carries memories, emotions and dreams, connecting the past and the future, tradition and modernity. In the dialogue of "Local and Individual Voices", poets believe that they are the guardians and innovators of language, and they should respect and inherit the precious heritage of local cultures and explore the deeper meaning of individual lives.

South African poet Vonani Bila argues that the popularity of English should not be at the expense of other local languages. Writing in the mother tongue is a manifestation of maintaining cultural identities and traditions, a direct way to communicate with the public, and a respect for linguistic diversity. He calls on writers to persist in writing in their mother tongue, bring unique value to literature, and show their own voices on the global literary stage. Ethiopian poet Seife Temam examines the evolution and development of poetry from ancient oral traditions to modern slam poetry. "Slam poetry" demonstrates the vitality and appeal of poetry in contemporary social life through time-limited competitions and on-site scoring. The performing, improvisational poetry "slam poetry" is not only an innovation in the oral tradition of poetry, but also an affirmation of the power of live words. Even in the era of digitalization and media dominance, live performances of poetry can still deeply attract and impress the audience. Indian poet Prithviraj Taur says that poetry is not only an artistic expression, but also a tool for transforming the world. Poetry is a product of exploration and questioning, and comes from a deep excavation of life. He believes that poetry can transcend time and space, express a deep understanding of existence, convey endless search and love of life, become eyes that witness history and enlighten the future, connect people's souls, and lead mankind to harmony and peace. Through his love for rural life and profound experience of nature, Chinese poet Liang Shuzheng explains that the true innovation of poetry should be rooted in the essence of life and nature, rather than just staying in the changes of surface language and form. Poetry should be a way to pay tribute to nature and life, providing consolation and redemption.

All four sessions of dialogues not only spark the poetry thinking, but also provide new possibilities for the exchange and mutual learning of literature, culture and even civilization.

诗与思：
缘于青春的对话与共鸣

　　青春有诗相伴，天涯于此共时。7 月 20 日下午，"首届国际青春诗会——金砖国家专场"学术对话如约展开，来自金砖十国的 20 位诗人相聚一堂，聚焦"诗歌的创新"主题，深入探讨了诗歌在当今世界的角色、功能、前景和创新的可能性与必要性等诗歌核心话题。

　　中国作协党组成员、书记处书记、《人民文学》主编施战军首先作了致辞。"或许，是青春在寻找诗歌，诗歌的模样就是青春的模样；反过来，诗歌也照亮了青春，爱诗的人永远年轻。"正是诗歌天然的促进沟通、增广交流的作用，将不同地区、不同信仰的人们聚在一起，包容世界的不同，弥合其分歧，丰富其色彩，达到"和而不同，美美与共"。施战军祝愿大家在此打开格局和眼界，结下友情和缘分，共同为促进世界诗歌的繁荣发展作出贡献。

　　《诗刊》社主编李少君和诗人赵四分别主持了四个单元的论坛对话。

诗歌修补心灵，探索万物诗意

　　5 位女诗人率先登场，围绕"生命的体认，爱与希望的色彩"单元主题展开对话。在她们看来，诗歌不仅是语言的艺术，更是心灵的抚慰。诗歌以原始而强大的力量，挑战着数字时代的浮躁，连接着人类共通的体验和情感，修补人们的心灵，传递着爱与和平的信息。

　　巴西诗人安娜·鲁什认为，诗歌作为一种人类原始的语言形式，具有挑战现代数字时代快速消费文化的力量。诗歌能够为看似无意义的事物赋予意义，表达人类深层的情感体验。21世纪的诗歌创新需要面对技术进步的挑战，利用技术来实现自身的发展。俄罗斯诗人叶芙根尼娅·乌里扬金娜相信诗歌本身就是对新事物的探索。她将诗歌比作"对未知的一跃"，是连接不同时空点的"虫洞"。诗歌的创新不在实验，也不在于寻找新的表达方式，而在于能否通过诗歌引导读者到达新的地方，带来变化和惊喜。埃及诗人娜贾特·阿里将诗歌看作探索万物诗意的冒险革新之旅。诗人要通过"重新衡量所有价值观"的行动，对抗封闭社会的传统观念。诗歌应该表达诗人的个人忧虑和问题，而非仅仅作为集体声音的传声筒。沙特阿拉伯诗人拉万·塔拉勒认为，诗歌如同一面镜子，反映着时代精神和个人生活的细节。诗歌的创新不应局限于形式，而应涵盖广泛的主题和内容，以适应不断变化的文化和技术环境，最终使诗歌成为连接人类共同体验和情感的桥梁。阿联酋诗人谢哈·穆泰里谈到，诗歌的语言不受地理和语种的限制，是全人类共通的语言。作为幻想与梦之主的诗人也应从生活的各种经历中汲取灵感，通过不断的自我更新和探索，创造出既具个性又能触动人心的作品。只有保持开放的心态，从不同的文化和生活中寻找新的视角和表达方式，才能真正激发出诗歌的活力。

诗人求新求变，追寻诗歌的荣光

诗歌的创新是什么？诗歌像一条河流，每位诗人都是这条河流的探索者，他们用创新的语言和形式，寻找着与世界新的对话方式。正如围绕"永恒即新，写诗就是创新"对话的诗人们所言，诗歌的革新不仅在于形式的探索，更在于其深刻的内涵和真实性，是它对美的展现、对善的胜利的信心。

巴西诗人蒂亚戈·庞塞将诗歌视作"卓越的书写形式"，指认现代诗歌总力图尝试语言的风险，以书写来沉思新。诗歌创作即一种新的呼吸方式，通过不断尝试文字、声音与意涵的结合和新的表达方式，以独特的声音与世界对话，建立新的联系，每首诗都是一次新的发现，一次对存在和语言本身的重新认识。俄罗斯诗人维亚切斯拉夫·格拉济林回忆了自己与老子《道德经》的结缘，认为诗歌真正的"新"不是表面的变化，而是触及诗歌内在的、永恒的"新"，他申言"永恒即新""真实即新""面向不可言说即新""优雅而朴素即新""严肃即新"，呼吁诗人们恢复对词语的敬畏，创作出具有深度和真实感的诗歌，以对抗时代的浮躁和浅薄。印度诗人尼基莱什·米什拉谈到，诗歌是连接个体与更大整体的桥梁，使人更加靠近家园。尽管技术发展迅速，但诗歌作为表达人类共同情感和经验的艺术形式，其核心价值并未改变。诗歌的创新深植于人类文化的根源和历史智慧之中，像在匮乏中进化的人类文明那样"生于忧患，死于安乐"，才能使诗歌葆有真正生命力。阿联酋诗人哈桑·纳贾尔通过回顾从古代到现代的诗歌发展，认为诗歌像天空一样恒久不变，其表达人类情感和经验的核心并未改变，变化的只是我们看待它的方式。诗歌真正的创新来自诗人的创造和想象力，既体现在构建诗歌结构的独特方式，也体现在诗人对现实的重新想象和连接。沙特阿拉伯诗人哈特姆·谢赫里认为，尽管小说是流行的文学形式，但诗歌以独特的方式连接不同文化、语言和世代的人，促进了共情和理解。诗歌以新视角看待世界，是一种深刻的自我探索工具，是重要的精神疗法，具有社会斗争作用，保护着语言和美学遗产，"诗歌是文学的珍珠，是永不老去的、庄重的长者……"。

创新是诗歌之神的主要武器

"诗歌之神能战胜新神吗？"围绕着这个话题，诗人们展开了深入交流和探讨。他们谈到，诗歌连接过去与未来、传统与现代，捕捉时代的脉动，诗歌之神的主要武器是创新，是深入人类精神世界的纯粹语言和形式。

埃及诗人谢里夫·沙菲伊认为，数字化不仅是技术层面的变革，更是一种全新的生活体验和感知方式，代表着时代的精神和哲学。数字化正在深刻改变诗歌的创作、流通和接受。诗歌新的增长点正在于深入挖掘数字化对人类生活的影响，探索诗歌与数字技术的内在联系。诗人要拥抱数字化带来的机遇。伊朗诗人基亚努什·汉·穆罕默迪回顾了诗歌面对的两次重大变革，一是动画的出现，经过了近两个世纪，诗歌之神已经能够让动画为己所用，表现形式的丰富性完胜动画。二是人工智能之神眼下向诗歌的进逼。截止目前，人工智能虽能够模仿甚至在一定程度上参与诗歌创作的过程，但 AI 算法创作的诗歌仍缺乏真正的创新性。诗歌之神的主要武器是创新，目前似乎还没有为 AI 所掌握。通过质疑艺术应该是什么样的固有观念，南非诗人阿尔弗雷德·萨弗尔谈及艺术属于公共领域，而它是否需要符合浪漫、政治或其他社会标签的期望，让他存疑。他认为诗歌和艺术能够揭示和批判现实世界的问题，激发情感、震惊和反思，这是艺术的真正价值所在。他提倡诗歌避免平庸和自我放纵，寻求新颖性，挑战观众的预期。伊朗诗人卡齐姆·瓦埃兹扎德分析了"发现"在诗歌创作中的重要性及其后续的探索和扩展，倡导诗人在发现之后，要进一步深入挖掘和创造，进行思维探索、拓展想象，建构更富有有机体质感的、带着现象磁场的诗歌文本世界。中国诗人胡桑表示，尽管现代生活趋向透明和便捷，但诗歌创作要有勇气探入对"真实"的深层体验，而非简单的叙事或复制。在数据流动的现代世界中，去探索更深层次的情感和意义流动性，让世界和诗人的主体流动起来，从而在数据时代找到独特的表达和价值。

母语为诗歌创作带来独特价值

本土还是国际，个体还是集体？诗歌承载着记忆、情感和梦想，连接过去与未来、传统与现代。在"本土和个体之声"对话中，诗人们认为，诗人是语言的守护者和创新者，要尊重并传承着本土文化的珍贵遗产，探寻个体生活的深层含义。

南非诗人沃纳尼·比拉认为英语的普及不应以牺牲其他地方语言为代价，使用母语写作是维护文化身份和传统的体现，是与民众情感交流的直接方式，也是对语言多样性的尊重。他呼吁作家坚持用母语创作，为文学带来独特价值，在全球文学舞台上展现真正属于自己的声音。埃塞俄比亚诗人塞费·泰曼探讨了诗歌从古代口头传统到现代砸诗形式的演变和发展。"砸诗"通过限时比赛和现场评分，展现了诗歌在当代社会中的活力和吸引力。表演性的即兴诗歌"砸诗"不仅是对诗歌口头传统的创新，也是对现场言词力量的肯定，即使在数字化和媒体主导的时代，诗歌的现场表演依然能够深深吸引和打动观众。印度诗人普里特威拉杰·陶尔表示，诗歌不仅是艺术表达，更是改造世界的工具，诗歌是探索和质疑的产物，源自对生活深层次的挖掘。他相信诗歌能穿越时空，表达对存在的深刻理解，传达对生活无尽的探索和热爱，成为见证历史、启迪未来的眼睛，并连接人们的灵魂，引领人类走向和谐与平静。中国诗人梁书正通过自己对乡村生活的热爱和对自然的深刻体验，阐述了诗歌的真正创新应当根植于生命和自然的本质，而非仅仅停留在语言和形式上的变化。诗歌应成为向自然和生命致敬的方式，提供安慰和救赎。

此次对话不仅碰撞出诗歌思考的火花，更为文学、文化乃至文明的交流互鉴提供了新的可能。

图书在版编目（CIP）数据

青春，如风有信 /《诗刊》社编. -- 北京：外文
出版社，2024. 8. -- ISBN 978-7-119-14038-4

Ⅰ. Ⅰ12

中国国家版本馆 CIP 数据核字第 2024T8K872 号

项目策划：陆彩荣　胡邦胜　施战军　邓　凯
项目统筹：张洪斌　李少君
出版指导：胡开敏

责任编辑：蔡莉莉
特约编辑：赵　四
助理编辑：马若涵
审　　定：熊　伟（葡萄牙语）　　郭大文（俄语）　　　贺　军（英语）
　　　　　李亚兰（印地语）　　　王　复（阿拉伯语）　王　浩（阿拉伯语）
　　　　　马　琳（波斯语）等　　（以外文诗歌出现顺序为序）
装帧设计：北京大盟文化艺术有限公司
印刷监制：秦　蒙

青春，如风有信

首届国际青春诗会——金砖国家专场

《诗刊》社　编

© 2024 外文出版社有限责任公司
出 版 人：胡开敏
出版发行：外文出版社有限责任公司
地　　址：中国北京西城区百万庄大街 24 号　　　　邮政编码：100037
网　　址：http://www.flp.com.cn　　　　　　　　电子邮箱：flp@cipg.org.cn
电　　话：008610-68320579（总编室）　　　　　　008610-68995875（编辑部）
　　　　　008610-68995852（发行部）　　　　　　008610-68996183（投稿电话）
印　　刷：北京盛通印刷股份有限公司
经　　销：新华书店 / 外文书店
开　　本：700mm×1000mm　1/16　　　　　　　印　　张：24.25　字　数：250 千字
装　　别：精装
版　　次：2024 年 8 月第 1 版第 1 次印刷
书　　号：ISBN 978-7-119-14038-4
定　　价：128.00 元